ON THE
SECRET SERVICE
OF HIS MAJESTY,
THE QUEEN

OTHER NON-BOOKS BY SOL WEINSTEIN*

LOXFINGER
MATZOHBALL

Abridged versions of *Loxfinger, Matzohball* and *On the Secret Service of His Majesty, the Queen* appeared in *Playboy* Magazine. Since the author has been informed that his sensitive masterworks of the real, the true espionage are popular with American servicemen, he would be grateful if his devoted readers would, upon completing them, send them to USO clubs, military bases, and hospitals, etc., instead of placing them in vaults next to precious jewels, furs and documents, or in time capsules, as so many have done. (Flattering, but unnecessary. Your sickening hero worship is ample reward.)

* A non-person

A THRILLING ADVENTURE OF
HEBREW SECRET AGENT OY—OY—7
ISRAEL BOND

ON THE SECRET SERVICE OF HIS MAJESTY, THE QUEEN

by Sol Weinstein

pb
SPECIAL
NEW YORK, 1966

DEDICATIONS

These include residents of NATO countries unfortunately omitted in the dedications to *Loxfinger* and *Matzohball*. What does it take to merit a mention in these towering novels? The answer is simple: Most of the people cited are not only cheerful, obedient, trustworthy and kind and never leave a national park without spraying their campfire embers with soft Culligan water, but also have gone out of their way to promote sales, thus insuring a better way of life for my fine family.

WILLIAM J. BLITMAN and NORMAN "RED" BENSON
In Memoriam.

ELLIE, DAVID (0010) and JUDY (007) WEINSTEIN
My fine family.

JOE E. LEWIS
Who once said, "Behind every beautiful woman is a beautiful behind."
If the Pickled Plato is performing in your town, don't miss him.

WILLIAM B. WILLIAMS
Of WNEW, New York. To the trade: Velvel Baze Velvel.

MERV GRIFFIN
Who gave me my first break on national TV. Merv, I still insist
that within my Walter Slezak-type body is a Sinatra-type voice.
Dare you ignore the commercial possibility of launching a Singing Spy?

NORMAN SHAVIN
Of the Atlanta Constitution; a geeter, a finer.

GODFREY CAMBRIDGE
Who, if the Bond film people ever decide to do
Live and Let Die, is the logical choice for Mr Big.

MAI ZETTERLING and SUSANNAH YORK
Who have been my constant companions in recent fantasies—
mine, unfortunately. Ladies, do with me what you will.

JULIE CHRISTIE
Take what's left.

TEX McCRARY

EARL WILSON

FRANK BOWERS

LEE J. MALTENFORT
Of Bestsellers.

JERRY AGEL
Of Books.

JACKIE FARRELL
Of the New York Yankees.

LEONARD KATZ
Of the New York Post.

FRANK FARRELL

WALTER WINCHELL

RON AXE & MIKE ROSENFELD
No female singer has the right to complain about the lack of good
material if she has failed to record "Mirror," lyrics by Axe, music
by Rosenfeld. It may be found in Vicki Carr's Discovery 2 *LP.*

LAURA LANE
A splendid song stylist.

THE NESHAMINY "N" CLUB
Of Bucks County, Pa.

ED JOYCE
Of "Expertise," WCBS, New York.

WALT CANTER
Writer and mensch.

JIM HARPER
Of WINZ, Miami, owner of one of the world's greatest picture names.
("Jim Harper, I can't ask you to go up against those rock 'em,
sock 'em Cornhuskers with a knee like that. So we'll lose
the twenty-third annual Okra Bowl; better that than crippling a
fine young boy forever." Jim Harper flashed his pain-tinged smile and
with the aid of a pneumatic drill the freckle-faced kid from
Glenville began to chip the cast from his leg. "Can't let
the guys down now, Coach O'Brien. Tell 'em to keep feeding
me on good ol' K-34 off left tackle. I'm gonna pack that pigskin across
those chalk lines until. . . .")

RAY HASSON and LIZ TROTTA
Of NBC News.

DIZZY GILLESPIE
John, there's still time to record an album of my modern jazz pieces.
Don't snicker; you didn't think I could produce top-flight thrillers, either.

GEORGE SPOTA
Of the Martin Goodman Agency, New York; with gratitude.

JOHN CALLEY
Of Filmways and the 99¢ Royal Roost.
Peewee Marquette, we never forgot you.

OSSIE DAVIS and RUBY DEE
Two elegant pros.

FLORENCE FRIEDMAN
Of Meyers Stationery & Book Store, Fairless Hills, Pa.
Sell, maideleh, sell. . . .

REGINA PRIOR
Secretary Emeritus to Johnny Carson.

CLARENCE PETERSEN
Of the Chicago Tribune, who looked into the heart of
a weary traveler and found cholesterol.

SOL IMMERMAN and BARBARA HUNTLEY
Artistic geniuses of Pocket Books.

BERNIE GROSS and MAX HUDES
Of the Carnegie Delicatessen, New York.

HARRY and JOHN HOLLAND

REGIS PHILBIN
Nobody should look that wholesome.

BUDDY GOLDBERG
Manager of the Jay Leader Insurance Team of the
Levittown, Pa., Western Little League, and his charges.

JESS CAIN
Of WHDH, Boston, an explosively funny, deeply disturbed young man.

ARNOLD BIEGEN
Of Booth, Lipton & Lipton, New York.

MELVIN L. KARTZMER
President, First Florida Consultants, Inc.

TEDDI KING and DAVID ALLEN
Fine pop singers.

JAMES J. SHAPIRO
Of Simplicity Patterns.

B. J. HARRIS
President of WQXT, Palm Beach, the "lebedicker from Louisville,"
and his PAULA, ALAN JON, PAMELA JOY and PEPPIE JAYNE.

LEON BROWN
Of the Philadelphia Jewish Times.

NEAL HEFTI
*Who, by his gorgeous reworking of blues, "Girl Talk," deserves the
chance to do the arrangements of my jazz pieces for an LP.*

JACK McKINNEY
Of WCAU, Philadelphia; seeker of truth.

SGT. NEIL ROBINSON
Of Armed Forces Radio.

DICK CAVETT and GEORGE CARLIN
Fine young comedians.

TIMMIE ROGERS
Who made "Oh yeah!" household words—in his household.

CASSIE PASSMAN, HARRY MOSES, LEN and NORA FISCHMAN,
MR. and MRS. ALBERT FINKLE, FRED and NETTIE BERK, CHARLES
and BELLA GREENBERG, CHARLIE GRAY, JERRY and MARY LOU
GLAZE, SAMMY MORRIS, FLORENCE GRAD LONDONER, CY and
CLAIRE NEIBURG, KENNY SOLMS, PETER REMENY, KENT TALIA-
FERRO, SANDY TIMMERMANN, MERLE RUDERFER, ESTELLE and
SIDNEY LUTZKER, JANET HELD, BOBBIE WEINER, MR. and MRS.
HARRY BOTOFF, MR. and MRS. NEIL LEVENSON, MR. and MRS.
ROBERT KURTZER, CHRIS WINNER, STEVE PINKUS, NANCY
CARTER, MENDY, WILLIE and DAVE KRAVITZ, MR. and MRS.
WILBUR J. LEVINE, STEVE SCHENKEL, DR. and MRS. MILTON
PALAT, DR. and MRS. GEORGE ISAACSON, TED and SYBIL COOPER,
ARNOLD and ESTELLE KIMMEL, NACHAMA LEVY, IRV and LEAH
WURZEL, HARRY BLAZE, MR. and MRS. WILLIAM GERVON, SY and
RUTHE LEDIS, FREDRICA KIRSCHNER.

FRAN SHANKIN

EVERETT G. WALK
Of Luden's, Inc.

JESSE H. WALKER
Of the New York Amsterdam News.

BILL (Talk of Miami) SMITH
*Of WKAT, Miami. Not a bad name, either. . . .
("You can kill me, Gestapo Chief Guttmacher, but there'll
be a lotta guys like me, Bill Smith, on the way . . . guys with
names like Tompkins n' DeLuca n' Kelly n' Weinstein . . . guys from
Glenville, Sioux City, Brooklyn n' Levittown . . . peace-lovin'
Joes who never asked for this war but when their Yankee
dander's up will show you how to finish a fight.
Hear those engines overhead, Guttmacher?")*

DICK WEST
Of UPI, witty but dewlapless.

OSCAR BROWN JR.
A delightful addition to anyone's record collection.

LES ROBERTS
Bright young writer.

HORACE GREELY McNAB
Of WBCB, Levittown, Pa.

RON POLAO
Of the unforgettable face.

LARRY DeVINE
Of the Miami Herald, *who, alas, never knew Yudel Kaplan.*

DONALD HAMILTON
Whose Matt Helm books never let the reader down.

"IAN STUART"
Sir, please kvetch out another Satan Bug, Black Shrike, *etc.*

ED BROWN, JUDY EDELMAN
and RUTH GOVER

ROBERT MAGAZINER JR. and JIM WILSON
Of Ocean City, N.J., officers of the first and
probably last Israel Bond Fan Club.

ROGER PRICE
Of Grump *Magazine.*

JUDITH RASCOE
With admiration.

WILLIAM H., JoANN and TERRI LYNN PETTIT
Of the Burlington County, N. J., Times

FRED E. WALKER
General manager of KYW-TV, Philadelphia.

NORMAN, MARGIE, MARSHA, SKIP and JANET WEINSTEIN
No relation, but worthy of inclusion due to sensible choice of surname.

WEINSTEIN'S DEPARTMENT STORE
Of San Francisco. Again, no relation, but the sign
just made me . . . kvell . . . all over.

NATHAN WEINSTEIN
Of Mystic, Connecticut.

MARYLOU SHEILS, BILL and LIL HOLSTEIN, FRANK and SUSIE MARRERO, ARNIE and PAT SOMERS, DR. HARRY LEVINE of 6360 Wilshire Blvd., Los Angeles, Calif., AL LEVINE of LONDON ASSOCIATES, Chicago, MAC and SHIRLEY ENGEL, EVE REMENY, JUDY

SPIEGEL, MARY JANE HIGGINS, MARETTA TUCKER, MR. and MRS. HAL SINGER, NORM LEIGHTON, NANCY HELPERN, MONIQUE VAUGEL, DOLORES MIRANDA, BERT and IDA ENGEL, STEVE PIERINGER, MIKE, SUSIE and TOMMY STUDNIA, STAN EARLY, ROSS HIRSHORN, NORVIN NATHAN, MR. and MRS. WALTER WARREN, MARVIN and PHYLLIS HABAS, MR. and MRS. SAM MELMAN, DAVID and ESTHER ZWEIG, LEONARD, HELENA PAVLOVA, LINDA, KAREN and SHERRY BOGARDE, JEAN BERNSTEIN, LINDA BILLINGTON, MARGIE, BERNIE and STEVIE HIRSH, DOLLY COHEN, MARY MILLER, SEYMOUR GINSBURG, DAVID and HOPE WISNIA, CARMELA CANDELA, BARRY SINCO, DAVID O'MEARA, TONY ROIG, CLAUDE and HEATHCLIFFE TRENIER, NANCY PALMER, pretty JAN and passable STAN FEINTUCH, LINDA LATZ, Bat Lady of San Francisco.

FRIAR BOBBY GORDON, MR. and MRS. FRED KANTOFF, PHIL WEISS of FRIEDMAN, ALPREN & GREEN, MRS. NATALIE FULTON, SELMA LITOWITZ, ALAN, GRACE, LEIGH, CORY and TOD BRESLAU, SAUL MILLNER, MURRAY HORNICK, MORTON SPITOFSKY, CHARLES CHARNE, ALLEN DELIN and the rest of BRONX COMMUNITY COLLEGE, NEWMAN and IRENE HOFFMAN, MR. and MRS. HAL LEFCOURT, GENE D'ANDREA of Andrea Motors, Morrisville, Pa., GEORGE and SARAH GORDON, PRISCILLA SLOSS, JAMES E. MAGEE of New York Life Insurance.

BILL HART
Of WCAU-TV, Philadelphia, who once stated, "No man is an island."
He also said, "No hockey puck is a dirigible; no telegraph pole is a
pencil box." Bill has this flair for correctly identifying things.

CEIL DYER

ANTHONY LaCAMERA
Television critic, friend of Norman Shavin.

GEORGE F. BROWN and EDDIE LOPEZ
Of the San Juan Star.

DAVE DUSHOFF, DALLAS GERSON and JERRY KATZ
Of the Latin Casino, Cherry Hill, N. J.

TONY BEACON and MARY MURPHY AIVAZIAN
Of the San Juan Diary.

WOODY ALLEN
With admiration.

LEON, CLAIRE and KIRK NUROCK
The last named an amazing young jazz player, arranger, composer.
Record companies please note.

DON THOMPSON
Of the Rocky Mountain News.

CLEVELAND AMORY
With gratitude.

HARRY NEIGHER
Of the Connecticut Sunday Herald.

WALTER BORENSTEIN
Of the North American Review.

JACKIE PETTYCREW
Of the Arizona Republic.

BEVERLEY GITHENS
Of the Eureka Springs, Ark., Times Echo.

DOLPH HONICKER
Of the Nashville Tennessean.

RUTH JACOBS and SHOLOM RUBINSTEIN
Of The Jewish Home Show, *WEVD, New York.*

SUE NAPIER
Of the Lexington, Ky., Sunday Herald-Leader.

RICHARD CROKER
Of the Georgia State College Signal.

CHARLES McHARRY
Of the New York Daily News.

JERRY GAGHAN
Of the Philadelphia Daily News.

FRANK BROOKHOUSER
Of the Philadelphia Bulletin. *In Philadelphia, nearly everybody
on the* Bulletin *reads* Mad *Magazine.*

HERB RAU

HERB KELLY

LENNY MEYERS
Of WHDH, Boston.

BILL and STUART BLUMBERG

JULIE DANE
*Of WHDH-TV, Boston. Noch a mool, the Name Game.
("What? Chili Chuvalo, the Chilean Spitfire, walked out on the*
Blofeld Follies of 1935 *ten seconds before the opening curtain just
because I wouldn't let her two-year-old brother conduct the orchestra?
Well, that does it—one million bucks down the drain!" Kindly old Pop
Abel Green looked up from his tattered* Variety. *"Now, hold on there,
Mr. Florenz Blofeld. Maybe you are the world's greatest showman and*

I'm just a broken-down old hoofer who sweeps up backstage, but there's a lovely young kid right under your nose, little Julie Dane, our script girl, and she's got a voice like an angel and she knows Chili's part by heart and. . . .")

HOWIE TEDDER
Of the Trenton, N.J., Times, who got me into this business. Blame him. (Ginmill comics who need shtik *should contact him.)*

CARL GEORGE
Of KABC-TV, Los Angeles.

NICK SERUBY
My old barber.

ELLEN WILLIS
Of Fact.

PAUL CONDYLAS
Of KABC, Los Angeles; "The Voice of the Tigris and Euphrates."

MIKE JACKSON
Of the Los Angeles Herald-Examiner.

BOB KENNEDY
Of WBZ-TV, Boston.

BRUCE McCABE
Of the Boston Record-American.

HERB KENNY and GEORGE McKINNON
Of the Boston Globe.

ROBERT TAYLOR
"The Roving Eye" of the Boston Herald-Traveler, *a likable, perceptive chap hamstrung by a prosaic name. Drop it; use Spangler Arlington Brugh.*

HELEN HESSEN
Nurse Parker at Duh Fontenbloo.

IRV KUPCINET

SAM BUTERA and ROLLY DEE

HARRY HARRIS, ROSE (SAM) DeWOLF and TOM LIPPMAN
Of the Philadelphia Inquirer.

GENE PACKARD and ART MILLNER
Of WKDN, Camden.

SAM GYSON

BEN McELVEEN

BEN BOROWSKY
Of the Bucks County, Pa., Times.

DAVID ROTHFELD
Of E. J. Korvette, Inc.

DEE CARUSO

ROBERT V. COX
Of Pepsi Cola.

DR. HOWARD S. FRIEDMAN
One of Philly's finest.

JAN MURRAY

KENNY DELMAR

ADAM WADE

JOHN WINGATE
Of WOR, New York.

ERNEST SCHIER
Of the Philadelphia Bulletin.

RAY JOHNSON and CHRIS GRIECO
Fine pianists.

MILTON THE FLORIST
Of Times Square Subway Florists, Inc. (IRT Division)

HARRY YAVENER, DOROTHY CANTWELL, ED "DUFFY" RAMSEY,
BUS SAIDT, LOU GUNKEL, HERB BLACKWELL, JOE LOGUE,
EDDIE HOFFMAN, STEVE MERVISH, PATTI PRINCIPI,
GEORGE MOLDOVAN
Of The Trentonian, Trenton, N. J.

ART THOMPSON
Of the Delaware Valley Advance, Bucks County, Pa.

BOB LANDRY
Of Variety.

MIKE CONNOLLY

WALLACE COOPER
Of the Associated Negro Press.

TOM STORY and DON BARNETT
Of American & Drew Furniture.

LADDIE SCHAEFFER, BERNIE COSNOSKI, BOB GOLDMAN,
DICK BURNS and TOM DURAND
Of WTTM, Trenton.

PEG MacEACHRON
Of WJNO, West Palm Beach.

WARD WILSON, MARY NEMEC and BOB WILSON
Of WEAT-TV, Palm Beach.

GEORGE WHITE and his SCANDALS—TOM ANDERSON,
BILL GORDON and SANDY LECHNER
Of WPTV, Palm Beach.

JAMES GARRETT
Of the Cleveland Press, *a nice man, even though he's the brother
of the polecat who gunned down Billy.*

GEORGE BARBER
Of WPBF, West Palm Beach.

PAIGE PALMER
Of WEWS-TV, Cleveland; Mrs. Strength and Health.

JOEL DALY
Of WJW-TV, Cleveland.

ED FISHER
Of WJW, Cleveland.

THE LINDELL A.C.
Of Detroit.

MARY MORGAN
Of CKLW-TV, Windsor, Ontario.

CAROL ANDERSON, FRED SHAW, MICHAEL THOMPSON and
JACK KASSEWITZ (a friend of Norman Shavin)
Of the Miami News.

DOC GREENE
Of the Detroit News.

MARK BELTAIRE
Of the Detroit Free Press.

LARRY JONES
Of WWJ, Detroit.

SHIRLEY EDER
Of WJBK, Detroit.

DICK OSGOOD
Of WXYZ, Detroit.

DICK DESAUTEL
Of WJLB, Detroit.

HAL YOUNGBLOOD, LEE MURRAY and JIM LAUNCE
Of WJR, Detroit.

THE SU CASA
Fine Mexican restaurant of Chicago.

JACK WALLACE and WALTER BLUM
Of the San Francisco Examiner.

EDDIE HUBBARD, JACK BRICKHOUSE and JACK ROSENBERG
Of WGN, Chicago.

JACK EIGEN
*Of WMAQ, Chicago, who does a trenchant, hilarious
impression of Mike Nichols.*

LEE PHILLIP and JUDY McKEOWN
Of the Lee Phillip Show, WBBM-TV, Chicago.

DICK BAKER
Of WCIU-TV, Chicago, America's greatest comedy team.

DUKE ZIEBERT
Of Duke Ziebert's Restaurant, Washington, D.C.

IRA BLUE
*Of KGO, San Francisco, the controversial gentleman for whom I
demonstrated my quicksilver ad lib ability by composing an
original song on the spot: "Ira Blue . . . Ira Blue . . . ain't
these tears in muh eyes tellin' you?"*

BILL GORDON
On the Scene at KGO-TV, San Francisco.

OWEN SPAN
Of KGO, San Francisco.

HILLY ROSE and BOB VAINOWSKI
Of KCBS, San Francisco, members of SPECTRUM.

JOSEPH P. MUNIZ
Of Thom McAn Shoe Co.

DON RIGGS and MARCY LYNN
Pittsburgh's "Wakeup Kids."

GEORGE BOURKE
Amusements Editor of the Miami Herald.

JAY BUSHINSKY
Of the Miami Herald.

LARRY KING
Of the Miami Beach Sun.

JOHN HAMBRICK and BOB HILL
Of KHOU-TV, Houston.

RIC RICHARDS and BOB KELLY
Of KTHT, Houston.

ARNOLD ROSENFELD
Of the Houston Post.

CHARLIE JOHNSON and ALAN JOHNSON
Of KPRC, Houston.

JEFF MILLAR
Of the Houston Chronicle.

BOBBY BROCK and BOBBY BRUTON
Of WFAA, Dallas.

DON DAY
Of KXOL, Fort Worth.

ED BARKER, WES WISE, JIM UNDERWOOD and FRANK GLIEBER
Of KRLD, Dallas.

JACK GORDON
Of the Fort Worth Press.

ANN TINSLEY
Of the Fort Worth Star-Telegram.

SID MARK, GEORGE LYLE, STEWART CHASE, JOEL DORN, VINCE
GARRETT, RICK FRIEDMAN, JOE ZAWACKI, GENE SHAY, RON
TILDON and ART (Bagels and Lox) RAYMOND
Of WHAT-FM, Philly's 24-hour-a-day jazz bastion.

BERNARD PEIFFER JAZZ TRIO
(Peiffer, piano; Johnny Coates Jr., vibes; Gus Nemeth, bass.
Fellas, I wrote these jazz pieces, you see. . . .)

CHARLES W. ADAMS
Of Coca-Cola.

LEO ARYEH ATTAR
Sportsman of Israel.

HUGH M. HEFNER, A. C. SPECTORSKY, JACK KESSIE,
SHELDON WAX, FRANK ATLASS, HY ROTH, BOBBIE ARNSTEIN
and TANIA GROSSINGER
Of Playboy. *"Hello, I'm your Bunny, Berigan."*

DOUGH CHINA, JAY STEVENS and MERRITT HADLEY
Of WGBS, Miami.

BERT WEILAND and JIM WHITTINGTON
Of WIGO, Atlanta.

FRANCIS RAFFETTO
Of the Dallas News.
(Recipe for a foileh verenik *furnished upon request.)*

VIDA GOLDGAR
Of the Southern Israelite.

TOMMY THOMPSON
Of WSB, Atlanta.

NATE ROBERTS and BERNARD BROWN
Of WGST, Atlanta.

HAL PARETS
Of KTTV, Los Angeles.

DAVE (The Pure American Voice) WEBSTER and MARY McGRAW
Of WQXT, Palm Beach.

OSCAR PETERSON and LUCKY THOMPSON
*Two great jazzmen just a furge of a fifkin away from immortality,
who could achieve it merely by recording an LP of
my . . . the hell with it! I'm sick of begging.*

* * * * * *

And, of course,

NANCY BROWN
Of Plainfield, New Jersey.

(If your name wasn't mentioned, there were valid reasons. Maybe you were a Don't-Bee, 'stead of a Doo-Bee, a Goofus and not a Gallant. But you have another chance because there's a fourth and final Israel Bond thriller in the works. So take that Dial shower every morning, warm the world with your tingly MacLean's smile and support your area National Educational Television station. I'll hear about it, don't worry. 'Cause you see, P. F. Flyers fans, Uncle Sol really loves you. He just wants you to come up to *his* standards, that's all.)

CONTENTS

"Don't Quote Me"—Bartlett

1. A King's Secret Shame

"Ben-Bella Barka."

The plea tugged its way past the swollen, blackened tongue through the desiccated lips.

The Grand Vizier of Sahd Sakistan looked down with pity upon the sprawled body of the man in the red Macadamia lizard nightshirt whose sweat-drenched head lolled against the virginal softness of the Doris Day foam rubber pillow.

"Yes, my King, O son of jasmine, honey and saccharin, blessed shining scimitar of ten thousand righteous disembowelments."

"Ben-Bella Barka, I am dying."

Ben-Bella Barka glanced at the fever chart stapled to the foot of the Norman Hekler-designed Bengalese ivory bed made of Consumers' Union-approved tusks from selected elephant graveyards. The jagged red line was at 119 degrees, the very top of the chart, and ended, still on an upward trend, at a notice which read: CONTINUED ON NEXT CHART.

"I fear as much, leopard of Araby. As it comes to all men in this uncertain world, so must the black camel of death come even to a king."

"Look, schmuck. Cut out the Westbrook van Voorhis *March of Time* documentary crap and listen to me," the king muttered. A sudden fit of coughing sent a trickle of blood down the right corner of his mouth. "Speak truthfully to me, Ben-Bella Barka, I command thee. What will befall my country upon my passing?"

Ben-Bella Barka winced at the king's choice of language. My master has been too often among the infidels, he thought. He tried to avoid the monarch's eyes as he answered. "Anarchy, O Lord of the Thighs, giver of pleasure to many concubines. You leave no heir. Thus, the Kurds and Wheys will be encompassed in a divisive power struggle, leaving Sahd Sakistan easy prey for the colonel in Cairo and his agents here. The mystery rider will do her best to save us, but who will listen to a mere woman?"

The king sighed. "Sarah Lawrence of Arabia, the beauty whose face no man has e'er seen unveiled." He coughed again more violently and groaned. "Ai! May Allah spray uncut Lysol upon all carriers of germs!

That last spasm split my truss. The end is nigh, my Grand Vizier. Is that cold fish of a German doctor within the walls of this room?"

"He is in the hallway beyond hearing, O roaring lion of a hundred Tom & Jerry shorts. Speak freely."

"Draw close. I shall divulge to you a secret which I have kept locked in my heart for twenty-seven years."

Ben-Bella Barka moved quickly to the king's side.

"I have a son."

"You jest, O panther of the bulrushes."

"Nay, I speak the truth. Listen well: Years ago when I was a young man given to wildness and adventure I heeded your advice when you told me to discard my royal raiments and go among the common people as a lowly seller of myrrh and frankincense so that I might learn something of the world outside the palace. I learned many things, Ben-Bella Barka, among them the fact that nobody in my kingdom knew what the hell myrrh and frankincense were and cared even less. In my absence you attempted to seize the throne and I was forced eventually to return and lop off your ears. Do you recall that episode, Ben-Bella Barka?"

"Louder, sire. As you know, I do not hear too well."

"During that one-year hiatus I became a merchant seaman on a charter boat carrying prostitutes from Calique to New York."

"Yes, sire. A tramp steamer."

"Good! You remember. In Manhattan, under the pseudonym of Bernie Seligman, I lived with a handsome, lusty Negro wench named Caldonia Simmons in a boisterous, fetid tenement at 117th Street and Madison Avenue, which, when it was finally condemned by the Board of Health as totally unfit for apartment dwellers, was converted by the city into an elementary school. Those were the happiest, freest days of my life, making uninhibited love to her three times a day and leaning out the fifth floor window to observe the colorful activities of the storied, high-powered Madison Avenue way of life; those distinguished men in smartly tailored grey flannel suits carrying attaché cases filled with heroin. But I digress. Caldonia and I had a love child, a boy named Beaster who has since taken his mother's name. I would have remained with her always except for her damnable stubborn streak and, thus, one night in a fit of pique I deserted them. She since has borne children by other men, according to our ambassador who was ordered to keep strict surveillance on the boy. A few years ago we lost contact with him. Yet, I know he lives. My son lives! And by the laws of succession he is the king. Find him, Ben-Bella Barka, and see he is rightfully seated upon the throne. Swear this by the beard of the prophet, Allen Ginsberg."

"This I swear, potentate of the pomegranates, master of ribbon-cuttings and shopping center openings."

Peace and resignation appeared on the shrunken face. "Ai! It is sworn, and should you abrogate this sacred vow Allah will dispatch myriads of locusts to clog thy giderum. In a little teakwood box under my pillow you will find more information pertaining to my son. As for me, Ben-Bella Barka, because I am an enlightened monarch, let my funeral be devoid of ostentation. I shall be buried in a plain platinum box and laid to rest inside a towering pyramid 10,000 cubits by 12,000 cubebs which need not be built by the blood and deaths of thousands but rather can be ordered prefabricated via the Spiegel catalog. Beside me will be my wives, bedecked in their finest Ceil Chapman black silk VC pajamas, my Cadillacs, gold and jewels, my stereo, my complete set of the works of Harold Robbins, and, for the love of Allah, please put in a humidifier. Ah, my faithful old jackal, I grow weary . . . the light grows dimmer . . . and yet I see a spectral face of infinite sweetness calling to me. . . ."

His voice grew faint. Then he pulled up his emaciated frame and stared across the room as though beckoned by a vision from another time, another place.

"Caldonia! Caldonia! What made your big head so ha-a-a-a-r-r-rd!"

He fell back.

Ben-Bella Barka, according to ancient Sahd Sakistani ritual, placed an Oreo cookie over each of the king's eyes and bound them to the skull with Tuck Tape.

King Hakmir Nittah Chinek, defender of the faith, protector of caravans and president of Mecca Records, was dead.

2. The Bitch Of Schweinbaden

Like an atomic fireball expanding in slow motion, the sun came out of the darkness, painting the Gulf of Aden gold. What had been a gloomy, foreboding shape by moonlight was transformed into a sparkling white villa on the shoreline of the Road of the Feculent Figs in the tiny enclave of Sahd Sakistan which clings to the southernmost tip of the Arabian peninsula.

The villa, ringed by hundred-foot high walls of Masonite-Dixonite, is known to the madcap international jet set as Shivs, the world's preferred gambling casino. Once the fifty-room estate of a sheik, it was confiscated by the Sakistani government during a revolution that saw the sheik flee to America and eventually become a paid consultant for the Joyvah Halvah Company. King Hakmir, desperate for funds to feed

his people, sold the white elephant to Hosmer Crenshaw and Mont-
pelier Melon, the safflower oil cartel barons, who, when they were
expelled from an exclusive London gaming club for not being able to
recite Kipling's "Boots," launched their own in retaliation. Under the
Crenshaw-Melon stewardship, Shivs began siphoning away the action
from the London club as well as Monte Carlo, Tangier and Darien,
Connecticut.

In the prime of their adventurous lives disaster struck these hearty,
Rabelaisian men in 1962. Their stylish two-seater went out of control
during Sahd Sakistan's fourth annual Soapbox Derby and hurled them
over a bluff into the sea. Because they had been the very spirit of Shivs,
it was assumed the casino would fold. It was saved on the day of their
funerals when the grieving widows, in a graveside transaction marked
by recriminations and a few well-placed blows with wrenched-off coffin
handles, sold Shivs to Heinz and Gerda Sem-Heidt, the husband-and-
wife co-chairmen of a mace-and-chain syndicate. The Sem-Heidts main-
tained Shivs' high standards while at the same time broadening its scope
to add skat, catch five, knucks, and pisheh-paysheh to the list of attrac-
tions which included "the big five,"—chemmy, baccarat, roulette, craps
and, of course—*la guerre.*

No matter how scintillating the play in the casino's other parlors, the
patrons were drawn by irresistible impulse at night's end to the *la
guerre* table. The moment of truth was here; all other forms of wager-
ing paled into insignificance. Only the truly affluent are found in the
La Guerre Room, for its membership is limited to holders of Account
Numbers 1 to 350 at the Suisse Bank de Legumes, which guarantees
personal cash deposits of no less than 500 million Bolivian *quasars* or
750 million Ruthenian *colodnys,* and any banker will tell you these are
the two most stable currencies on earth.

At 11 A.M. the doors to the conference room at Shivs swung open,
admitting nine of its ten directors. They seated themselves in plush
Norman Hekler-designed Jamaican poisonwood chairs with matching
ottomans and lit aromatic Muriel cigars. There were two places at the
head of the table for the co-chairmen—one empty, the other more than
amply filled by the corpulent bulk of Heinz Sem-Heidt, who signaled
for silence.

"Since our voices can be heard on the sound system in the cellar and
my wife can converse with us, we will proceed with the agenda. Herr
Zentner?"

A tall blond man with watery eyes stood ramrod straight. "I have the
pleasure to report that King Hakmir is dead." There were murmurs of
approval, even handclaps. "We, of course, have sent word to the palace
that the directorship of Shivs offers its heartfelt condolences (laughter)
and regrets that the valiant efforts of our physician, Dr. Ernst Holzknicht, to save His Majesty, were to no avail. (Louder laughter.) It was
most fitting that the good doctor should have attended the king, for it
was he who placed the *sivana bacillus* in the king's Diet Pepsi in the

first place." The directors gave a standing ovation to the smiling doctor, who shook his head with self-effacement.

"A minor but hardly insoluble problem has evolved. From a listening device planted on the fever chart we have learned there is an heir and that Ben-Bella Barka has been ordered to seek him out and enthrone him. The Grand Vizier will be shadowed, of course, and Hakmir's son eliminated by some regrettable accident. We foresee a rulerless enclave beset by a vitiating power struggle between the Kurds and their traditional enemies, the Wheys, enabling our client from the U.A.R. to take control. Our fee will amount to 900 million *quasars,* plus 10 percent of the royal treasury."

Herr Zentner sat down to sustained cheering.

An iron voice cut through the collective self-satisfaction and their smiles vanished as though wiped off by an artist's brush.

"What about the mystery woman? I want her eliminated!"

Heinz Sem-Heidt blanched. "Mein liebchen, Gerda, we are doing all in our power to end her disruptive tactics. I swear to you by Himmler's pinky ring that before long she will be rotting in the sun."

The iron voice in the cellar was cold, dripping with malice: "This Sarah Lawrence of Arabia, as she calls herself, for the last year has been preaching unity between the Kurds and Wheys, appealing for an end to antipathy for the sake of Sakistani nationalism. She has led them in sorties against U.A.R. infiltrators. She even urges them to enter upon friendly relations with Israel." A stream of curses followed. "Who is she? Why is she here? Is she in the pay of the Zionists? I want these answers and the issue resolved immediately!"

Heinz Sem-Heidt collapsed in his chair, his obscenely fat jowls shaking. "You have heard my wife, gentlemen. Put a Condition Black priority on Sarah Lawrence of Arabia. We will hear other reports. Herr Krug?"

"Fellow directors, I wish to report that our fee for capturing Hebrew Secret Agent Moe Zambique, Oy Oy Five, taken in Damascus and brought here for questioning by Gerda, will net us twenty-five thousand Straits dollars when we turn him over to Syria."

"Twenty-five thousand Straits dollars?" There was rebuke in Heinz Sem-Heidt's retort. "A pittance. The capture of an ordinary Double-Oy from Israel's M 33 and ⅓ is worth easily five times that figure. And if we had taken Oy Oy Seven, well. . . ." His hands made a sky's-the-limit gesture.

Stocky Herr Krug puffed his Muriel. "Yes, but this should be considered what the Americans term a 'loss leader.' Let the Syrians have him for that price. They will soon become so highly dependent on TUSH, our Terrorist Union for Suppressing Hebrews, that we can safely raise the ante on each succeeding job."

There was a long trailing scream from the cellar. As inured to violence as they were, the nine men shuddered.

The iron voice returned: "Gentlemen, let us not concern ourselves with the piddling Syrian payment. Oy Oy Five will be of no use to them now. Please delay any further items until I come to the conference room."

They heard the whine of the elevator, then the doors opened and a wheelchair bearing Gerda Sem-Heidt was pushed across the green-and-black swastika-patterned carpet by a dwarf in a dunce cap and a medieval jester's outfit with tinkling bells on his pointed shoes.

Gerda Sem-Heidt fixed her mustard-yellow eyes upon her twitching husband, then let them scan the other directors. She was a wizened crone of seventy-three who bore a startling resemblance to the witch in the cartoon *Snow White*. Her hands were bony, clawlike, empty of rings, with extra-length fingernails which the dwarf set about honing to razor sharpness with sandpaper. Her face was chalk white, which made the yellow eyes and vein-blue lips appear even more hideous. Virtually bald, she concealed her few wisps of yellowish-white hair with a fiery orange Larry Mathews wig. Her cadaverous body was covered by a red and white Robert Hall housedress and her unstockinged, bean-shooter feet were ensconced in Kitty Kelly's Mexicali Rosen *huaraches*. And there was something else on her body, revealed by the deliberately opened housedress.

As the directors saw it their sullen Nordic faces turned a sickly greenish hue. She watched their reactions with a smile. No matter how many times she displayed it, they could never become used to it.

Gerda Sem-Heidt was the proud possessor of a plastic heart.

Dr. Holzknicht alone was undisturbed as he viewed with clinical detachment the exposed components in their transparent styrene housing, the action of the atria and ventricles, the unoxygenated blood changed to bright red by the lungs. It was he who had installed the device after a seizure that left Gerda paralyzed in both legs and close to death. The plastic heart drew its power from an external electromagnetic coil hooked into a transistor battery that never left her lap. The same coil toasted her English muffins of which she had a constant supply in her pockets. Now she grew bored with her shocking little game so she closed her housedress. "Let us continue, gentlemen. I want to hear Dr. Holzknicht's summation of 'Operation Alienation.'" To the dwarf: "Locksley, a muffin, *bitte*."

Dr. Ernst Holzknicht, a slightly built man with a bland face and the large forehead of the scholar, cleared his throat. "Fellow directors, as you know, I am not only a surgeon but a diplomate of the Schisselzelmknist Institute of Advanced Psychiatry. It was my good fortune to assist occasionally our Führer (the men's right hands shot up in a robotlike heil) during those phases of the war that called for an understanding of the mentality of the Third Reich's enemies. When our beloved co-chairmen, Heinz and Gerda Sem-Heidt, whom we all served with unquestioning loyalty in those glorious, fulfilling days at the Schweinbaden Concen—er, Detention and Cultural Rehabilitation Center—asked me to mount a plot against the *Juden*"—several of the directors growled; Gerda spat into Locksley's puckered apple of a face —"I accepted their challenge with strength through joy. In our previous sessions we have discussed the psychological factors which are involved in 'Operation Alienation.' Now it remains only to carry out the physical extirpation of these installations"—his hand swept across a map of North and South America and Western Europe containing thousands of locations denoted by pins—"and Phase One will be complete. Then in a few days we should begin noticing the inevitable results. Thousands of field men will be taking surveys on synagogue and Jewish organizational attendance, United Jewish Appeal contributions, Catskill Mountains and Miami Beach resort bookings, El Al aircraft and Zim Line cruise ship reservations, etc. I have not the slightest doubt that we shall witness a drastic decline in all of these activities. Now I shall yield to Heinz Sem-Heidt, who will outline the personnel problems."

Heinz Sem-Heidt pushed his hands down hard on the armrests of his chair to hoist up his three-hundred-pound body. "There are no personnel problems, mein lieber Doktor. In this world, happily, there is never a shortage of Jew-haters. (Laughter and applause.) It was a simple matter for our sub-agents who combed the locations marked on our map to find disgruntled individuals willing to attach a Calgonite charge to the wall of a Jewish-owned business. There are five thousand key targets on the three continents, which means the total cost to TUSH, at one hundred dollars Amerikanische per incident will be approximately a half-million dollars. My winnings at *la guerre* alone should cover that cost.

"It is an ingenious plan and we are beholden to our dear colleague. The repercussions felt by the State of Israel will avenge TUSH for many indignities, not the least the murders of our dear Führer (the men heiled again) and our top assassin, Torquemada LaBonza, at the hands of Secret Agent Israel Bond. Our stock will rise on the Espionage Exchange when the Arab world observes that we have caused the virtual withering away of Israel and Judaism without resorting to armies, nuclear weapons or germ warfare. And, as a not inconsequential subsidiary benefit, we shall enjoy the destruction of M 33 and ⅓, the Israeli secret service, and M., the disgusting old harpy we now know is its Number One. And who knows? If Wotan and Thor are smiling down on us, Oy Oy Seven will also be found in the rubble. Gerda, my sweet, do you have any comments to make?"

"Put the plan into being." The blue lips smiled, but there was no mirth on the face or in the mad-dog yellow eyes. It has been a most satisfying day, she mused. A Jewish agent hangs from his thumbs dead in the cellar; my dear doktor has crafted a plot to bring the verminous Jewish state to its knees. A most satisfying day. . . .

For a moment she seemed years younger, "The Bitch of Schweinbaden" of the happy, rewarding days. It was not for nothing that those few who escaped her clutches to tell the tale never referred to her as Gerda. To them she was and always would be "Auntie" Sem-Heidt.

3. Trenton, I'm Coming!

Executing a picturebook LeMans turn, he swung the majestic old 1938 Vance-Packard, the automobile of true status seekers, over the instep of the CITGO attendant, shouting, "You're a gasser!" as the man fell stricken against the high-test pump (the witticism, he knew, would do much to assuage the pain from the mashed foot) and headed out of the restaurant stop onto the New Jersey Turnpike. Destination: Trenton, New Jersey, place of his birth.

Israel Bond was going home.

The meal had been as exciting as a Blue Barron recording of "Tiptoe Through the Tulips." There was no doubt in his mind; the world's safest job was that of a foodtaster for Howard Johnson's. No, don't be smart-alecky, he scolded himself. The dessert, frozen baked beans on a stick, had been first rate, the coffee rivaling Horn & Heartburn's best, and the painting of the waitresses' faces orange and turquoise to conform to the general decor a cheery touch.

A surge of power from the Vance-Packard, whose 24-cylinder, 8.6 axle ratio, short-stroke, tall-coxswain engine was revved up to maximum cruising speed of 118.9 hectares, sent a chill pulsating through his being. With no strain it hummed past two Cadillacs and an Imperial (all parked on the shoulder for repairs), its 12-ply Firestone tires purring a symphony at that most crucial of the world's rendezvous—where the rubber meets the road.

Bond stuck a Raleigh between his sensual, Chap-Sticked lips and adjusted the magnifying glass on the Vance-Packard's visor to entice a goodhearted cosmic ray to veer from its endless course toward galaxies unknown and zero in on the cigarette's tip and ignite it.

His two-week vacation after the El Tiparillo affair* had not been prosaic. An old love, Charlene Krosnick, had stolen away from her husband and children to share a night of bliss with him in New York. He took her to see *The Bantu and the Bubby,* the musical comedy sensation by top songsmiths Manny Sheldon and Sheldon Manny about a sweet Jewish grandmother who convinces South Africa to abandon

---

* *Matzohball,* Pocket Books Inc., 1966, $1. It contains certain insights no Ian Fleming novel could ever hope to match.

its odious policy of racism and appoint a sensitive Negro goatherd as its new prime minister. They dined at romantic, candlelit Nedick's where a strolling gypsy comes to your table to play your favorite *chansons d'amour* on his tambourine as the waiter pours the orange drink over ice shavings. She then insisted he take her to see *Thunderball,* the popular spy movie. "Gosh, Iz," she sighed as she gazed into the mocking yet tender grey eyes of the secret-agent hero on the billboard. "He kind of looks like . . . you. Are *you* really some dashing spy, Iz?" She giggled at the thought. "I hardly think a guy who promotes Mother Margolies' Activated Old World Chicken Soup would be a swashbuckler, though, would you?" And on an impulse and to tease him she kissed the figure on the advertisement.

"You're making me jealous, Charlene," Bond had jested. "But I'm better than he in one place," and he whisked her via subway to his luxurious suite at Manhattan's regal Ansonia Hotel where he whispered, "Let there be no puerile shame, no holding back. *Every pore must score.*" As their bodies fused in *score de combat,* he crooned into her fragrant apricot of an ear an aphrodisiacal song based upon the Kama Sutra.

> *"I'll be loving you, all ways . . .*
> *"With a love that's true, all ways . . ."*

But he had become bored with matchless ecstasy so he had accepted two part-time freelance jobs. The first had been a puff. Through Seymour Feig, an old drinking buddy, he was engaged by a Mr. Farraday to fly to Los Angeles and bring back a certain package. He went there without incident via the "friendly skies of United" (Pan Am's were indifferent; TWA's downright hostile, he had been told) but coming back a charming girl in the adjoining seat turned out not so charming after all, covering him with a Chase-Manhattan .38 Banker's Special and expressing an interest in his attaché case. He had been compelled to drive the case against her lovely jaw, breaking it and disabling an operative from the second leading weekly news magazine in America. Back in Manhattan he delivered the flat parcel to the soft-spoken, pipe-smoking Farraday, an agent for the Number One such publication.

"Capital, Mr. Bond! Now, until we release it ourselves, the secret of who will grace our magazine's 'Man of the Year' cover is safe, thanks to you."

He had refused Farraday's sizable check. "I cannot in good conscience accept payment. My people owe you an everlasting debt. Your magazine's recent, heralded Essay on Judaism with its generally favorable tone has done more to secure recognition and acceptance for my people than any document since the Ten Commandments."

After a lump-in-the-throat silence during which he realized he was in the presence of a unique human being, Farraday said, "Is there anything we *can* do that might please you, Mr. Bond?"

"One trifling favor. Have your Show Biz editor do a nice, lengthy feature piece on the gentleman who has taken it upon himself to be my Boswell and chronicle these adventures of mine. And now, sir, may good *Fortune* attend you and may you have *Time* to enjoy it!"

Farraday cracked up. "Geez, that's hilarious!" and when Bond, eyes atwinkle, zinged in a topper, "Of course, don't play fast and *Luce!*" he'd literally fallen on the floor.

Assignment Two had been no piece of cake, his torn shoulder testified graphically.

"There's a frightened kid holed up in the Hotel Bogaslovsky on West 46th Street," Bond was informed on the phone. "He's promised to work for us, but if he steps out of that room for sure he'll be killed."

"Who's after him?" Bond wanted to know. It was the kind of question a real top-drawer agent asked.

"There are undercovermen in town representing cliques from Dallas, Minnesota, Philadelphia . . . many others. They're ruthless men and if they can't have him, they swear nobody else will. They tried once in Chicago, even killed his guard, but he slipped 'em. Deliver him to us alive and usable and there's twenty grand in it for you. Use the code words 'Flood Formation' and he'll let you in."

The terrorized tot, Bond discovered, was one Casimir Predpelski, aged twenty-two, six feet six, 275 pounds, from Hamtramck, Michigan. Bond spent the better part of a day calming the thumb-sucking Gargantua in Dr. Denton pajamas with a medley of Polish love songs, which included "A Glass of Beer, a Bowling Ball and You" and "Keep Throwing That Dart, in the Dartboard of My Heart."

A chunky little room service waiter named Paulo Gunty brought matters to a head. As Bond noticed with relief from the third-story window the van that was to take him and Predpelski to freedom, the little waiter held out a huge candy cane to the lad. "We always bring some sweets and goodies to our younger guests. It is a policy of the hotel."

"Candy! Candy!" the monster cried with a childish eagerness that made Bond smile a parental smile.

Click!

In a hideous second of revelation Bond knew the truth. Two feet of naked steel shot out of the cane brandished by the little man in the monkey jacket who had played the servile fool until his victims were lulled into complacence. Gunty shouted a fanatical "From Green Bay with hate!" and thrust at Predpelski with the classic *coup de murville*.

Bond hurtled his frame between swordpoint and bobbing Adam Nowicki's-apple on Polish throat, incurring a nasty slash as it ripped through the trenchcoat epaulet down into his right shoulder. But he'd yanked out the Chris-Keeler, squeezed the trigger and heard the characteristic, silencer-muffled *slut! slut!* and saw two angry holes pop up in

Gunty's forehead. There was an insistent hammering at the door and someone shouted, "Break it in."

Undoubtedly there were more of Gunty's cohorts in the hallway, perhaps far too many to handle.

When he saw the stuff in the corner, an inspiration flashed through his mind.

It was piled up in an odiferous mound.

Kielbasa!

The Polish sausage the kid loved best. Links and links of it. Holding his nose, Bond tested the links. Good-o! They were bound by solid, dependable Bangalore twine.

"Here's our escape route, buddy boy," he told the whimpering leviathan. "Tie one end around the bedpost and throw the rest out the window."

He put two more slugs through the door, exulting in a scream. He heard a voice: "Jesus, he just killed the chambermaid."

Bond looked down. Predpelski had already shinnied down the thick, greasy chain of sausages with amazing agility for one his size and was bolting into the back of the van. Bond started his own descent, his long, tapering fingers around the links in a viselike grip. He was at the second story now, pausing just long enough to chance upon a disrobing brunette and take her phone number, when he spotted the trio of hired killers racing up the street to the van.

Swegroes!

They were the flaxen-haired, lapidus-lazuli-eyed, chocolate-hued descendants of Swedish mariners who decades ago had impregnated the willing women of West Africa's Hullaballuba tribe. They wore Libby's split-peajackets, nail-studded Levi Strauss Levi's and crepe-soled Aleutian bedsocks. Once, on a psychological warfare mission into Jordan where he had dynamited a theater showing an Omar Sharif movie, Bond had come in contact with a Swegro, disguised as an usher, in the employ of the Jordanian league for actors-in-espionage, Mosque & Wig. It had been a hellish minute of combat that left the Swegro decapitated and quite incensed about it and himself with a dirk in his shoulder. A mean lot, Swegroes, far worse than Bulgars, and now he had to get past three of them!

They saw him immediately. Shots rang out, one of which skinned his gun hand and he dropped the Chris-Keeler into the street. *Gottenu!* Unarmed!

There was one chance. He kicked out against the sign HOTEL BOGASLOVSKY, MANHATTAN'S PREMIER RESIDENCE FOR DRIFTERS AND INDIGENTS and, releasing the chain, fell through the roof of the van, crying, "Go! Go!"

Miles away, the van parked at Yankee Stadium, the driver handed Bond the twenty Big Ones. "You've pulled it off, Mr. Bond, but then, it's what we'd expected of a man with your reputation. As for you,

Predpelski, sign here on the dotted line. Thanks to Israel Bond, young fella, you are now the middle linebacker for the New York Giants."

There could have been a third freelance gig, for even bigger money, but Bond had no desire to tail the president of General Motors.

A burst of song from the Vance-Packard's custom-made Atwater Kent UHF-CIO radio drove the perilous Predpelski affair from his mind. It was a composition that had moved the hearts of Americans from coast to coast and was certain to capture the annual Larry Hart Award for the most meaningful lyric of the year.

"Batman!"
"Batman!"
"Batman!"
"Batman!"
"Batman! Batman!"
"Batman!"
Unforgettable!

For variety's sake and Abel Green's as well, he switched stations.

". . . on record against this evil manifestation of man's inhumanity to man. Mass murder is bad business. It is degrading to its victims. It by no stretch of the imagination does anything to dignify the mass murderer. It removes from society people who have a vast potential in many areas. It causes resentment, economic dislocation, suffering and sorrow. Mass murder must end and that is the unequivocal policy of Station WDULL here in Metuchen, New Jersey. You have just heard our fourth radio editorial condemning mass murder. Of course, any responsible spokesman with an opposing viewpoint will be given equal airtime to reply."

He changed stations.

". . . extraordinary series of events. Following the mysterious explosion that leveled Wishnevsky's famous bagel and bialy bakery under the Jerome Avenue El in the Bronx come reports of like explosions or bombings—though no deliberate criminality has been yet proven—throughout the country. Two famous Kosher wine companies have had their Brooklyn distilleries blown to bits with three known dead, seven missing and scores injured. Traffic in that unhappy borough is backed up all the way to Michigan City, Indiana. In Manhattan two prominent show business delicatessens on Sixth Avenue went up, hurling tons of sour pickles and tomatoes through a stage door onto the Rockettes at Radio City Music Hall. In Coney Island a convoy of trucks transporting Nathan's immortal hot dogs has been wiped out on the Belt Parkway. Chicago's contribution to the holocaust has been several explosions at bakeries, wine warehouses, dairy product plants and three huge corned beef and pastrami processing centers. Windy City police said the sky there looks like Mrs. O'Leary's cow is back in business again. Here's more: like events are occurring in Philadelphia, where a cream cheese plant and dozens of small delicatessens and a number of catering houses were blown up; St. Louis, Detroit, San Francisco,

TRENTON, I'M COMING!

Cleveland, Denver, New Orleans, Miami Beach, the last named a shambles . . . in short, every major city in the U.S. Reports of additional explosions in all of these cities are coming in so fast the news wires are running behind. There are further reports, unconfirmed, that several major cities in Canada, Western Europe and South America have experienced disasters at the same sort of establishments. A freighter of Panamanian registry, the *Hispianola Roll,* en route from Halifax to New York, radioed news of an explosion and a raging fire in the hold. Coast Guard vessels are steaming to the rescue; helicopters have airlifted seventeen wounded. We will interrupt for further bulletins. Now back to William B. Williams and more of that great WNEW sound of music."

For the next half hour Bond relaxed as William B., he of the humorous, dulcet voice, spun some of the Chairman of the Board's greatest vocals from albums dedicated to young lovers, swinging lovers, medicare lovers, liver lovers, etc. If he had not been so enchanted by the music he might have surrendered to a nagging voice inside (or possibly outside; one could not be sure where nagging voices came from unless one were hopelessly married) that urged him to think, think, think about the bizarre newscast, seek some grand design in the widely spread catastrophes.

The sign on the Trenton Freeway bridge said "SLIPPERY WHEN WET," followed closely by one that said "NOT SLIPPERY WHEN DRY." The on-the-ball New Jersey Highway Department would let no driving condition go undescribed, an impressed Bond thought.

He pulled into the driveway of his brother Milton's town & country clubber at 1919 Starling Dropping Drive in the heart of Trenton's opulent Hiltonia section, and parked behind Milt's snappy 1966 Sherpa-Hunza. He banged the solid brass Rusty Warren knocker against the massive Pacific Plywood door. It opened and he was bathed in the love and warmth of home, the not-too-sister-in-lawly kisses of Lottie, the whoops of leaping Rickey, twelve, and a mushy buss from adorable, six-year-old Praline. Milton himself stood strangely apart; a questioning look said: We've-got-something-to-discuss, younger brother.

4. "My Boys, They're Killing My Boys!"

"LET HE WHO IS WITHOUT SIN BEGIN SINNING BECAUSE HE'S MISSING FUN! FUN! FUN!—Mother Margolies."

The long queue of sun-baked tourists waiting to be admitted into the various divisions of Mother Margolies' factory outside of Tel-Aviv noted with approval one of her typical Old World proverbs emblazoned on the main gate. "Gosh, eighty-four years old and she still comes up with those golden thoughts," said a B'nai B'rith president from Wisconsin, fanning his pink, flushed face with Joel Lieber's authoritative *Israel On $5 A Day*. "I wish we were in there already," responded his wife. "I'm dying to get hold of her personal recipe for Mother's Activated Old World Clam Chowder." Her husband snorted. "Don't you know the first thing about the dietary laws? Clams ain't Kosher; they don't chew their cuds. . . ."

In the private, sealed-off wing of the factory M. watched the throng on her closed circuit TV as she knitted what soon would be Oy Oy Seven's new paisley shoulder holster. A *geeter boychik,** that Israel Bond, a little sex crazy sometimes and maybe a little too clothes conscious, but when it came to murdering and maiming, a fine person altogether. Oy, such a dirty business this cloak and dagger stuff! What a shame good upstanding fellows like Bond and the rest of the Double Oys had to expend their talents on these nefarious activities when they could be raising families and studying our holy works. But nations must have security forces or they succumb to predators. It's the way of the world, I suppose, she reflected. I've lost my own dear nephew, Nochum, in this filthy enterprise.

M. was worried, deeply so. With the exception of Bond, who was on leave in the United States, all the Double Oys were unaccounted for. Oy Oy Five had gone to Syria to track down a lead on these TUSH people and had failed to call in. If he'd been taken by TUSH and that . . . that *thing*, Auntie Sem-Heidt, heaven help him! In M.'s way of thinking, TUSH was as dangerous to the survival of her nation as

---

* Good boy.

34

the American Council for Judaism. Now Double Oys Two, Three, Four and Six were missing—and right here in Israel! They had gone to that little bureau near the Ministry of Defense in Jerusalem to renew their licenses to kill . . . and never returned! She'd sent the new lad, Neon Zion, to investigate. Where *was* he?

And what was the meaning of these explosions bannerlined in this morning's Tel-Aviv *Trumpeldor?* They all seemed to have occurred at Jewish establishments in both the Old and New Worlds and many of them were somehow related to eating and drinking. Certainly, food for thought.

All in all, it was a gloomy day, she thought, putting aside the completed shoulder holster and starting on a trenchcoat for Lazar Beame, her chief of operations; for Israel had just lost a potential friend, King Hakmir of Sahd Sakistan. An Arab, true, but not one of the diehards. Through his Grand Vizier, Ben-Bella Barka, he had made overtures of a peaceful nature to Israel's ambassador in Paris.

The day wore on. She watched the tourists, Americans for the most part, meandering through the Potato Lotke division, the Hall of Kishke, and the new Schaveria and shrieking with delight at the automated conveyor band carrying pots of fresh-made beet soup—"The Borscht Belt," as Oy Oy Seven had named it. What a wit that lad had!

The buzzer sounded. "M., it's Quartermaster HaLavi to see you, sir," said M.'s beauteous secretary, Lilah Tov. "Shall I send him in?"

"Yes."

"Oh, sir. Have you heard anything about the Double Oys? Op Chief Beame is most concerned."

"As yet, no. But the one you're personally concerned with—" M.'s TV focused on Lilah's blushing loveliness—"is safe, Miss Tov. Oy Oy Seven will be back soon."

Lavi HaLavi walked through the door. "Shalom, M. I have come to discuss some new devices for the field." He was an intense, nervous little man with fidgety eyes that seemed afraid to look into hers. The white-laboratory-coated QM had been back in harness just a few days, having spent the last six months at Foam Rubber Acres, the Service's rest home for distraught personnel. "Oh, I can't stand it in here!" he cried. "This cold air drives me insane."

"Patience, HaLavi," M. said in a tranquil tone. "It will be quitting time soon."

"I have added some new modifications for Oy Oy Seven's car, the Mercedes-Ben Gurion." He spread open a chart. "You will notice this, Button 71-a. If Bond is being tailed he has only to press it and a movie screen rolled up in a rear bumper springs out, a camera emerges from the roof and projects a series of . . . uh . . . shall we say 'art films' . . . which cannot help but distract any members of the 'oppo' in the car behind, thus giving him time either to eliminate or capture them, as the situation dictates. The films were taken by me at Bond's request and deal with his summer-long escapade with the Countess Tracy Di-

Terrazzo-Crotchetti at Portofino. Ever the sexual perfectionist, he uses them as training films to study techniques, manipulations, and so forth. They would make a ballistic missile come to a dead stop."

HaLavi lit a Raleigh and tore the coupon from the pack, placing it in a receptacle near her desk. "My ninth contribution of the day, M. You should soon have enough for that nuclear reactor. To continue; Button 95 releases a mist of Colgate's 007 cologne to freshen both his face and any wilting carnation in his lapel. And I rather think the Colgate copywriters missed out on an obvious grabber of a slogan that would treble their sales: 'Use 007 Products and You, Too, Will Get Pussy Galore.' Button 96 pops a piece of Danish into his mouth; 97 converts the MBG's front grill into a barbecue pit into which 98 flings filet mignon for two, seasoned, to be sure, with Accent; 101 converts his license plate into a hilarious sign that says 'CHICKEN INSPECTOR'; you know Oy Oy Seven's far-out sense of humor . . . and 105 converts any *shikseh* riding with him into a member of our faith by a tape cartridge containing recorded instructions for instant proselytizing and a spray symbolizing a ritual bath. Oh. . . ." he pinched his nose. "This air conditioning. . . ."

"Go on, Quartermaster HaLavi."

He dragged on his Raleigh. "I have taken the liberty of sending Oy Oy Seven several new portable devices in care of his brother in Trenton." From a pocket he fished out something. "This is my new anti-homer capsule capsule. If Bond suspects an enemy has swallowed a homer capsule, he needs only to introduce the anti-capsule capsule into the other agent's body and it will nullify the first one immediately. Here's a little toy he will find invaluable." HaLavi held up a length of metal. "It is a device which can be strapped to his leg. I have urged him to carry it at all times. Made in my laboratory by a fantastic new process of freezing ore at one million degrees below zero, its ridges can slice through any metal known to man. The new metal, by the bye, is called Instant Processed Cold Rolled Extra Strength Steel."

"Excellent, QM!" She nodded. "Now you may take a breather from the air conditioning. Shalom."

Gasping, his nostrils flaring in his anxiety, HaLavi fled. Then a chill shook M.'s body as she heard Lilah Tov cry, "3-D! 3-D! 113 is back with a 3-D!"

3-D! Danger, doom, disaster!

Neon Zion, 113, was a pale young blond ghost as he slunk through her door. "Dead. All dead . . . Oy Oys Two, Three, Four and Six. They were in a cab on Ben Yehuda Street after leaving the license bureau. It blew up." He sobbed and buried his face in her shawl.

"My boys, they're killing my boys," M. said, keening, close to fainting.

At that moment the homeward-bound receptionist, rummaging among the coats in the front-office cloakroom for her own, found the thing under M.'s silver-blue mink, ticking, ticking, ticking. . . .

5. Those Vines Have Slender Shapes

Milton Bond at forty-five was twelve years older than his Israeli brother. Like all the Bond men (there was a third brother, Ragland, forty-one, a Jonny Mop quality control inspector—"Rag" to everybody), he was blessed with the familial dark, cruelly handsome visage, his bloated a trifle by dietary indiscretions. The Bonds were Russian Jews who had settled in Trenton after a decade in London's East End where the father, Solomon, was employed by the local branch of Youngtwerp of Antwerp as a rhinestone cutter.

After the passing of their parents and the departures of Israel and Rag Bond for their own careers, Milton had wooed and somehow won Lottie Vine, one of the lithe, leggy, desirable daughters of industrialist Oleander Vine, and with the father-in-law's backing opened a successful catering house in West Trenton, the Pinochle Royale, where upper-class Jews staged their various social and sometimes religious functions.

Throughout Lottie's sumptuous meal Milton remained uncommunicative. She noticed this and attempted to brighten the occasion with light banter. "Trying some new things tonight, Iz. Mrs. Paul's frozen fishsticks, Mrs. Paul's frozen shrimp, Mrs. Paul's frozen mythical kraken suckers. . . ."

"What's the next thing she's going to freeze? *Mister* Paul?" It was one of Bond's better jests, yet he noted Milton's face held no smile. Something wrong there. Milton normally would roll on the floor for that kind of a one-liner.

"Okay, big brother, noble patriarch of ye Clan Bond." It was a few minutes later and he was emerging from a bracing shower with Mione Soap, its haunting flavor permeating through Milton's bedroom. "Let's have it, stoneface."

Milton sat on the edge of his Norman Hekler-designed Xochitl tostada bed, puffing doggedly on a 95-cent Houdini. "Your face. It looks like hell. And your body—bruises, welts, slashes. It's like this every time you come home for a visit. What the hell are you doing for a living, Iz? And no crap."

Bond inhaled a Raleigh, blew a figure eight the hard way—four twos. He looked into those grey eyes, so shrewd and hard like his own. "You know what I do, Milt. PR for Mother Margolies. These"—he ran

37

his hands over the purple and yellow blotches—"are the result of a car crackup."

"That scar on your shoulder?"

"If you want to know the truth, Adolph Hitler did it to me. With a Luger."

"I said, cut the crap. I've had the feeling for a long time you're in some kind of . . . well, undercover stuff. PR guys don't get chopped to pieces from parroting the praises of chicken soup to adoring women on seven continents."

Seven. Milton said *seven.* My number! Does he know even more than he's suggesting? Of course, there *are* seven continents; he would have been idiotic to say "twelve."

Bond's face stiffened. "Why don't we just watch a little TV, huh?" He flicked on the Zenith portable, giving an affectionate pat to as many of the superior, hand-wired circuits as his long, tapering fingers could locate.

When the buzz died down an Indian chief, hatred blazing from his lined face, spoke: "White man steal Apache land, white man slaughter buffalo, white man make Injun loco with firewater, traumatize him, emasculate him, steal Indian nuts, leave him rootless without something of value. Now, white man—die!"

The rangy trail boss did not flinch. "Hear me, Running Abscess, mighty chieftain of the Trocadero Apaches. You and your braves massacred the peaceful homesteaders at Lamprey Landing, took many scalps, burned homes, schools, churches, trading stamp redemption centers. And now you expect the Great White Father in Washington to put your likeness on the new nickel after *this?*" He drew the trembling woman in calico to his breast. "I'm savin' one bullet for you, Miss Lucy. I seen what these murderin' redskins do to white women." She cringed. "What—what do they do, Lonestar?" He looked at his boots in embarrassment. "They . . . they violate 'em, Miss Lucy." She screamed: "Yoo-hoo, dear sweet Apaches! Over here! Over here! Take your goddam hands off me, Lonestar. . . ."

Milton turned it off. "Iz, I want you to do me a favor. I want you to see Lottie's sister tonight. She's been asking about you."

A pang triggered a sonar ping in the soul of Israel Bond. Liana Vine! Youngest of the desirable, leggy, lithe daughters of Oleander. She remembered.

They had been "The Sweethearts of Trenton High" and, on a few hundred fumbling occasions and seventy distinctly competent ones, lovers. Cool, lissome, blonde Liana. Probably there had been three or four prettier girls that year . . . Phyllis Rosenblum, the cattle dealer's daughter; Monique Introlligator . . . mischievous Felice Pixie Berman. But there had been something special about Liana, something you couldn't put your finger on (it was rare in that respect). Her painfully shy smile? Perhaps the gliding carriage of a ballet dancer? Or maybe it was the protective urge she evoked in him, the way she made him feel she *needed* him as he posed her for pictures against the gate of her father's hundred-acre plastics factory.

It might have come to something, but then erupted the trouble in Palestine. Young Israel Bond, steeped in intense Jewishness by his parents, heard the call for deliverance from across the world. He had long been involved in Jewish National Fund collections, he belonged to Young Judea, Trenton's YMHA,* the Allenby Club and A.Z.A., a fraternity for Jewish high schoolers with mathematical interests (Angle Zide Angle).

With alacrity he joined a kibbutz† near Hightstown, N.J., where Zionist-minded youths were being trained to endure conditions approximating those in Eretz Israel, fabled land of Milk and Magnesia. Realism was the keynote at K'far K'Near, once the potato farm of McSorley Shinn, a taciturn Baptist. The eager kibbutzniks slept on straw mats in barracks swarming with scorpions and pit vipers (imported at great cost from the Holy Land), tilling the soil under fire. (The kibbutz had advertised in a rural weekly for men who wanted $1.25-an-hour work shooting through barbed wire at Jewish boys and girls. K'far K'near had been overwhelmed by the generous response from the surrounding community. Many had expressed a willingness to perform this service gratis, proving, as a highly complimentary article in the kibbutz newspaper pointed out, that brotherhood was no myth.)

The war. Awful moments on mountain roads pocked by mortar shells. Hand-to-hand combat with bestial mercenaries of Glubb Pasha's Arab Legion. His rapid rise in the informal yet deadly Palmach** to the rank of water carrier. A flair for recklessness and conspiracy noticed by an astute colonel in the Shinbet,†† leading to an eventual post with M 33 and ⅓, the coveted Double Oy number and a license— to kill!

Eighteen years away from Liana. Still she remembered.

There was a small PR chore to get out of the way, a speech before the Histamine, the ladies auxiliary to the local chapter of the Histadrut,*** which met each month at the Pinochle Royale. Then the decks would be cleared for an evening with Liana. Her voice was silky, teasing, on the phone. "Mother and Daddy are in Aruba, so it's just you and me, Iz. Wear something casual."

"Like my skin, dearest?" He prayed she would not hear the juvenile pounding of his heart.

He donned a pair of Botany 1,000 nankeen stretch pants and Shropshire Argyle bedsocks, and pulled a buff-colored cashmere T-shirt over his rippling torso. He completed the ensemble with a multiflowered Korvette's luau car coat of guazeroy and went downstairs, six steps at

* Young Men's Hebrew Association.
† Farm settlement.
** Army of Israel.
†† Major intelligence apparatus of Israel.
*** Zionist Labor Organization.

a time, to meet Lottie's admiring, "Wow! Is someone I love very much duded up sharp to meet someone else I love very much!" The oval face softened. "Iz, be kind to her."

There was Praline to kiss goodnight, but not before she recited a poem she'd memorized "just for you, Uncle Israel." Whereupon she launched into Robinson Jeffers' "Roan Stallion," faltering here and there as a tyke might, but giving it a generally knowledgeable reading. "Off to bed, you rascal!" and he whacked her saucy behind. For Rickey, who was above that sort of thing, a catch with the lad's new Superball, a five-minute tutoring session on the New Math ("X can lift 60 tons of potash; Y can lift twice as much potash as X; Z can lift only half as much as X. Question: Why is Z avoiding his social responsibilities?"), a hearty handshake and "keep studying for that Bar Mitzvah, fella."

A good kid, Rickey, with the usual problems of adolescence. "Uncle Iz. Dad's kinda corny about some things, so can I talk to you about, uh. . . ."

"Don't do it, Rickey lad. You'll go blind and eventually insane. You shouldn't be troubling us oldtimers for advice, anyhow. That's the kind of thing you should be learning on the streets. Tell you what, fella. Uncle Iz'll send you some Superman color slides that'll explain the whole thing. These were made in pre-Castro Cuba. 'Night, Rickey."

In Milton's Sherpa-Hunza they made some safe small talk about cars, politics, suburban life. "Pretty quiet out here," said Milton with satisfaction. " 'Course we did have our little excitement last summer. Guy next door's power mower went mad. One minute it was breezing along chewing up the crabgrass; next minute it whacked out, ate up three poinsettia beds and somebody's pet Schnauzer. When it went for a Volvo we got scared, called the SRS . . . that's the Sears Rescue Squad . . . and they shot the poor bastard dead on our lawn."

"Any of that wife-swapping bit going on out here?"

"Nah, old hat. The real hippies are swapping their mistresses. Hey, Iz, did you read Jim Michener's new book?"

"You bet, Milt. Damn fine. I saw him in Jerusalem while he was gathering 'Source' material."

From Milton's outraged "ooooh" and his howls of hilarity Bond knew the ice of early evening had been broken.

Chums again!

6. "The Martini Gave You Away . . ."

He finished the speech before the sweet old matrons, any one of whom could have been fated to head the Secret Service of Israel, so much like M. were they. Having won Mother's products a few dozen more lifelong supporters, he rejoined Milton in the latter's modernistic, Norman Hekler-designed office with the genuine Peruvian Tupperware spittoons which were gaining favor with busy executives.

"Come on, Iz; I'll take you through the joint."

He led the Israeli through the Pinochle Royale's rooms, explaining their functions. "You see what it is, Iz. Jews have become so jaded; they just won't buy the oldtime ways any more. You gotta give 'em that ol' show business pizazz in every area of existence. Now this," and Milton's eyes were humorous, "is the Slice O' Life Room."

No further explanation was needed as Bond watched the rite of circumcision performed upon an eight-day-old squeaker in a room whose walls were a montage of *Life* Magazine covers. *"Noch a Yid!"** Bond said with fervor. "Amen," Milton chimed in. As the *mohel* worked, they saw the child's cowering father, his arm before his face. Not so the mother, who coolly applied a tape measure to the pink monkey feet.

"Real Jewish mother," Milton commented. "Already measuring him for corrective shoes."

After they passed through three kitchens ("Kosher, non-Kosher, Kosher-style," Milton informed him), they came to a masculine den upon whose knotty pine walls hung pennants of Midwestern universities and photographs of elephantine football players with grim expressions (Bond spotted Casimir Predpelski in the togs of Michigan State). "This is our Big Ten Room."

"For old grads and such?"

"Hell, no. This room is for the minyan.† Hence the name. Clever, huh? The Tanteh Claus Room is undergoing repairs so we'll skip that one."

"Tanteh Claus?"

* "Another Jew!"
† A Jewish religious service requiring a minimum of ten adult males.

41

ON THE SECRET SERVICE

Milton stripped the tinfoil off a 95-cent Houdini. "Well, you know how our kids feel sorta deprived when Christmas comes around. So I dreamed up a great *shtik* that's made this place the talk of the East, maybe the country. We have this little old lady in a red dress and white beard sit on a throne in that room and the kids come in and tell her what they want for Chanukah. If they've been real good, she says she'll drive up from her big Lincoln Road toy shop in her Cadillac, which is jammed with goodies, and leave 'em Chanukah gelt and toys for eight straight nights. The parents are wild for the idea 'cause this way we work in religion. Now, my magnum *epis*."

They walked through nutria-lined swinging doors into a vast nightclub setting crowded with raucous people in furs and evening wear. "It's bigger than the Copa, huh, Iz? This is the Club Thirteen, my room for post-Bar Mitzvah receptions. Got a dilly tonight for multi-millionaire Keefe Barrington's kid, Whitney. Getting this shindig was quite a plum in my compote. Every fency-dency catering house in the East was after this one."

On stage at the microphone an animated little man in a flashy Crawford Clothes Po Valley mohair suit was gabbing.

"Good evening, ladies and germs. Welcome to Whitney Barrington's Bar Mitzvah reception. You know what a Bar Mitzvah is. That's when a Jewish boy reaches manhood. And a motel is where he proves it!

"And speaking of San Francisco . . . I just wrote a song called 'I Left My Heart in San Francisco and My Sinuses in Arizona.' "

He spoke through a cupped hand to the musicians. "Notice how the hip material never makes it? Well, back to the dreck, by heck. My wife is a lousy cook. She has to call a repairman to fix a TV dinner.

"Jesus, it's *all* dying tonight. And is she square? She thinks a condominium is something a guy buys in a drugstore.

"Speaking of spies, they got a lot of spies on TV. There's a new spy called Blue Light, but he's got troubles. Whenever he drives his car they won't let Blue Light cross at the Red Light until they give him the Green Light!"

Marvelous, marvelous, Bond thought, envying the clever construction. Why aren't these fools laughing? And haven't I seen this little funmaker before? Yes. It was Henny Benny Lenny, West Coast comedy sensation. His mind wandered back to a night at the Kahn-Tiki, the leading Class B hotel in the Catskills, and pain twisted the cruelly handsome face as he recalled the wonderful girl who had been so enmeshed in that electrifying Loxfinger caper,* the girl who now slept under the eternal sands of the Negev. Poontang Plenty. Something cried out from the core of his being with the profoundest sincerity: *Better her than me.*

"Speaking of sex, did youse hear about the Greek who found true

* *Loxfinger,* Pocket Books, Inc., 1965, a magnificent overture to this unsurpassable series—S.W.

42

love by accident? He backed into it. Oh no, this can't be the *regular* Bar Mitzvah crowd. My kid likes rock n' roll. His favorite song is 'I'm Too Tired to Rock Around the Clock, So Let's Just Walk Around a Watch.' Forget it, you f—— rich-bitch bastards!"

Wow! Bond enthused. What a great powerhouse of an impromptu shock line, designed, of course, to win back the blasé celebrants; but they continued to ignore the scintillating monology that could have been theirs. He jotted down as many of Henny Benny Lenny's gems as he could remember.

Henny Benny Lenny's triangular head hung in defeat.

"And now," he blared, "the real star of this show, Master Whitney Barrington!"

As the 25-piece band crashed into a pounding, frug-beat version of "Mahzeltov!" the crowd broke into yells at the entrance of a small boy with an incurious, bored demeanor who walked down a red carpet toward the stage flanked by six dazzling young women in extra-tight diamond-encrusted miniskirts. At a signal from Henny Benny Lenny six cages descended from the ceiling into which the maidens sprang.

Whitney Barrington, resplendent in a Steve Lawrence formal turquoise quilted lounging robe, midnight-blue Dean Acheson diplomatic trousers with sateen stripes and regimental Martin Agronsky patent leather loafers, squeaked out of his world-weary face from a voice box whose nodules were pimple-stippled:

"My Bar Mitzvah speech."

Bond nudged Milton. "Bet his dad's grinning from ear to ear right now."

Milton grimaced. "The old man ain't even here. He's an Ethical Culturist. It's the *shikseh* he married who insisted on the Bar Mitzvah."

Something odd happened. After his opening line, Master Barrington's voice suddenly became rich and dramatic as the lips moved hesitantly, droning on about "my sacred commitment to the faith of my fathers" ... "this memorable day in which I take my place among. ..."

"Hell," Bond grunted. "That's Richard Burton's voice. The kid is lip-synching his speech."

"Family's got money, Iz." Milton shrugged. "Whose voice do you think sang the selection from the Haftorah* in synagogue this morning? Robert Merrill."

Whitney Barrington's proclamation of his covenant with the ancient faith concluded, Henny Benny Lenny raised his hand and the band hit a fanfare; the girls frugged tigerishly in their cages.

"Now, ladies and germs, the presents! Will the gentleman from Price Waterhouse please come forth . . . or even fifth . . ." (the sharp ad lib died) ". . . with the envelopes?"

Bond left somewhere between the 500 shares of AT&T from Uncle Giles Rivkin of West Palm Beach and the "12 points, Whitney, 12

---

* The additional reading from the prophets.

points in Uncle Morris Barrington's Shalomorris Hotel in fab-yew-louse Lust Ve-e-e-egaa-a-as!" Weary of it all and sorry for Master Whitney —it's all downhill for him after tonight, he thought—Bond needed a drink, but not here in this Fellini orgy scene. "Try any of the kitchens; there should be someone around. Place's full of part-time help tonight," Milton said.

The man behind the service bar in the Kosher-style kitchen was tall, powerful and very blond, very cruelly handsome, too, Bond noted. He looks like a Gestapo me.

"Hungry, old chap? Or thirsty?" The accent was slightly German, the English colloquially good. "We have just the sort of fare that will appeal to your discriminating taste buds, Mr. Bond. Gold-speckled-with-mauve bayou heron eggs, scrambled, not shirred, pommes de terre Chevelle, piping hot Chase & Sanborn Coffee—and remember, sir, what Mr. Chase didn't know about coffee, Mr. Sanborn didn't know, either—served with Domino Sugar's Vitali-style cubes cut to geometric exactness by Cal Tech-trained technicians. . . ."

Bond lit a Raleigh. "How did you know my name was Bond? And that my tastes are so extraordinary?"

The blond man smiled. "You must admit, sir, you look remarkably like the entrepreneur of this establishment. And you hardly seem the sort who'd order Skippy peanut butter on white bread."

"You're very perceptive. A Montessori Martini, please."

The man set about making one. "Beefeater Gin made from potatoes crushed by the feet of exceedingly bright Italian orphans, a Samuel Bronston lemon, and a little shake. . . ."

Bond's heart was about to burst through his splendid chest. He smelled it on the man's large, corded hands. Calgonite! The thoughts piled up like blue chips on a la guerre table. Calgonite. Bombing. A Calgonite-scented man in a Jewish establishment. Jewish establishments being bombed left and right. And the last three words. . . .

He smiled in spite of himself. "The martini gave you away. Martinis are stirred, never shaken. Anyone who drinks 'em shaken is a social misfit. And I saw the tattoo on your wrist when your tuxedo sleeve moved up . . . the symbol of the SS jackboots kicking naked buttocks. You're from TUSH."

7. Candy, I Call My Killer Candy

"Sessue Hayakawa!"

The Nazi spat it from his sneering mouth as he hunched into the ping-pong stance of the karate expert.

It's started, Bond thought. He's attempting to "psyche" me with a stream of vitriolic Japanese words that will bring on panic, terrifying images of him as the star pupil in the Ginza studio of Sensayuma, "The Cobra," master of unarmed combat.

I must "psyche" back, guttural word for guttural word, hissing curse for hissing curse, until he, too, is beset by devilish eidolons of me as a holder of the Black Belt in the top half of the twelfth Dan, in my red Dan River karate robe, the star pupil of Moto of Sausalito, the only man alive whom Sensayuma fears. And I must be *all* Moto; a mere quasi-Moto will not intimidate him.

Hunching into a similar pose, Bond snarled:

"Ginza! Osaka!"

"Nagasaki! Hiroshima! Hirohito!" The TUSH man's rejoinder was disdainful.

Gottenu! Three Japanese words in a row! Does this kraut really know the lingo? No, Bond, don't use "lingo" when you yell back. It isn't even close. He'll die laughing of contempt.

"Ko-Ko! Yum-Yum! Kyoto! Saki! Sedaka! Glocca Morra!" There, Hun! Six straight! But those last two . . . true, they *sounded* legit, but will he accept them? Or insist on the strict rules laid down in Admiral Yumekimi Meshuga's definitive *Pre-Karate Combat Cursing?*

The TUSH agent yawned, a great comical yawn.

Gottenu! He treats this as though it's a kindergarten exercise! Is he *that* confident? There is an unnatural stillness in the air, the moment before the black funnel springs out of the west to carry away the Kansas farmhouse, Dorothy, Toto. . . .

In a quicksilver instant the German cried: "Zero!"

"Mostel!"

Oh, *Gottenu!* The response had been mechanical, unthinking. Israel Bond, you stupid son of a bitch! You fell into the oldest trap in the game. He knows you can be had. Round One to the killer from TUSH!

The smell of victory in his nostrils, the blond titan soared off the balls of his feet, his stiffened Commando's cutting edge of a right hand smashing down on Bond's torn shoulder . . . screaming: "Fukuoka!"

Bond fell back growling a savage, "Same to you oka!" but his paralyzed shoulder was a useless instrument. A brutal savate kick to the stomach almost bent him double and sent him crashing into a service stand, spilling a trayful of dessert over the marble floor; another to the same spot and it was all over. He lay groaning, conscious of two Flagg Brothers pebble-grained brogues planted at each side of his neck. One sickening thought kept pushing through the red haze in his head:

I've been taken by a man who wears nine-dollar shoes!

Standing over him like a Colossus of Rhodes was the scarcely winded man from TUSH. Why doesn't he end it? Stupid question, Oy Oy Seven. These TUSH people are never content with a mere "hit." It must be accompanied by the infliction of total degradation. I know what he has in mind for me.

"It is finished, Oy Oy Seven. I had long entertained the hope of ending your career in this fashion but the co-chairmen of my organization had already contracted to furnish Torquemada LaBonza to the KGB to do the job. Alas for him, happily for me, he was not equal to the task. In a few seconds I shall kick your head off its trunk, then plant a 50-zis Calgonite charge that will blow this Jewish pigsty to oblivion and 300 sons and daughters of the Chosen People with it, including your beloved brother. It is the kind of thing I have been doing for the last twelve hours in New York as part of Dr. Holzknicht's magnificent 'Operation Alienation.' As an added fillip, I may leave another 50-zis at your brother's house. His sweet children will enjoy the ride. And now, the crowning touch, *Judische-hund*. . . ." There was a clicking sound of cubes. "Drink your martini—shaken!"

He'd known it was coming, but that didn't make the ignominious, nauseating stream of ice and liquid on his lips any more bearable.

But there was *something* bearable, something with prongs pressing into the small of his back. Something that could be a weapon. He must keep drinking the martini to glut the TUSH man's appetite for sadism. He felt his gorge rising but he kept swallowing. His left hand was inching under his back. Now!

"Fork you!"

It tore out of his throat with maniacal fury as his left hand drove the fork into the TUSH man's ankle, savoring the awful wail as prongs chomped through skin, capillary, gristle, marrow, cockle, mussel and bone. The German was howling like a banshee, writhing on his own back now like an animal in a trap. Bond yanked at the fork. Stuck too deep! His hand closed on a hard, cold object near the spilled tray and he drove it into the horrible O of the screaming German's mouth, past the palate, hammering it with his elbow far back into the throat, snapping off six gold-filled teeth in the process. There was an eye-rolling paroxysm, the face turned a revolting purplish-blue, the hands flopped at the sides.

Out of curiosity Bond forced open the jaws and extricated the object that had killed by strangulation. A thin smile hardened the cruel, sensual mouth. To no one in particular he remarked mildly, "There's nothing like a frozen Milky Way to take those snotty Snickers off a face."

Oblivious to the swelling on his head, the gushing shoulder wound and the fire in his kicked stomach, he frisked the German, found a plastic I.D. card:

"James Bund, 43, Ulbricht Allee, Schweinbaden, D.D.R."*

So this was James Bund, Number Two in TUSH's murder gang and one of the Schweinbaden camp ghouls as well. Bond found an interesting notation elsewhere on the card:

"Religion, Druid."

As a man not only licensed to kill, but also to perform a memorial service over the victim (when possible), he felt obligated to perform the latter function, even though the man had been a swine about the martini. But . . . Druid? He summoned to mind the only appropriate liturgy he knew to cover this situation. He whispered:

> *"I think that I shall never see,*
> *"A poem as lovely as a tree . . ."*

Then the martini finally got to him and Israel Bond was very sick.

8. Dark Pool, Sweet Pool

He found the Calgonite in a Volks in the Pinochle Royale's darkened parking lot, shoved the corpse of James Bund into the back seat and drove deep into the woods of nearby Titusville. With a makeshift fuse of Bund's shoestrings he touched off the Calgonite, and from a hill a half mile away watched the blast sear 300 feet of scrub pine. The "pineys," those moonshiners of the forest, would be blamed for the explosion, he was certain. He could almost hear some rural sheriff cackling: "Them stupid bastards made the white lightnin' too damn powerful that time. . . ."

Using his European heel and toe walk (which he had been taught by

* East Germany.

a European Olympic champion with but one heel and one toe) he ate up the six miles back to Liana's house in twelve minutes, using the time to reflect on the fast-moving events since he'd heard the newscast. The phrase "Operation Alienation" kept bedeviling him, but for the second time in the same day he repressed an analysis which might have led him to something concrete, for he was now standing before something very concrete, the Vine mansion at the corner of Lazy Lazarushian Lane and Molting Macaw Road. It was a fabulous edifice designed in the Early Guy Madison ranchero period by the Finnish architect Rynno Duren, whose intelligent use of Saran Wrap, stalagmites and pumice stone highlighted a score of striking brothels in Kansas City.

The door was open. A silvery voice said, "In the kitchen, Iz," and he tiptoed across the Dacron-Orlon-Leon rug (the latter no miracle fibre—the manufacturer wished merely to immortalize his son) and. . . .

There was Liana Vine.

Naked.

She stood braced against the Progressive Furniture Company's Totie Fields model table, proud, unashamed, fully cognizant of the effect of her wondrous physiognomy upon him. "If anything's to happen, dearest Iz, it should be in here. No matter how rich we get, we Jews still live in the kitchen."

"I'm hungry," Bond said. "Did the special pie I ordered from Maruca's come yet?"

Without warning she began to cry, her creamy shoulders shaking. "Oh, it's all wrong. This whole thing I had in my mind . . . seeing you after eighteen years . . . and I'm naked . . . and all you're interested in is some damn pizza pie. . . ."

He slapped her hard. "Sorry, *ketzeleh,* but I don't dig hysterical broads. Not even one I love with all my heart." The last sentence, pitched in a low, throbbing tone, seemed to snap her out of her funk and she dried her face on a rich-textured, high-pile Hudson napkin. "Besides, Liana, you're a Trentonian and you know damn well we call it *tomato* pie, not pizza. And only Maruca's of 119 South Olden Avenue refuses to pander to commercialism by utilizing provolone or mozzarella, two flat, uninspiring cheeses when cold, let alone melted. The Maruca boys, Pat, Jake, Spike and Slippery Joe, top their pies with their own secret formula, the only other copy of which is in a Curia safe in Vatican City."

"You've changed, Iz." Her smile was sweet yet grave. "You're so sophisticated n' all." Her warm, finely fleshed but not disgustingly plump arms encircled his neck. "Were there others, Iz?"

His fingers caressed the silky Chemstrand hairs at the nape of her neck. "Don't throw up smoke screens, my pet. The question isn't what *I've* been doing. I'm a man. How about you, *maideleh?* Simon pure all the way?"

Her breath titillated three of the 1,917 erogenous zones on his left ear. "Just once, Iz. It was back in '57 and I hadn't gotten a letter from you in nine years and . . ."

"Tramp!" He shoved her against the wall. "You bitches! You're all alike. Who was it?" His slaps turned her cheeks blood red.

She bowed her head. "A guy I met at the John Cage Music Festival in Poughkeepsie. He was the third player in the coal scuttle section. Short, fat, morose fella . . . kinda reminded me of comedian Jackie Vernon. I was just sorry for him, Iz, 'cause everybody was dancing with a girl and he was dancing with a cello, and I guess I was sorry for myself, too. Nine years without. . . ." Her voice cracked.

His nose rose, pushed up by a snarl of loathing. "And now you want your old lover boy to swing for you a little, eh, bitch! By heaven, I'll take you as callously as I took . . ." He reeled off four thousand different names, each one a dagger in her heart, he knew.

Arms flailing like a John Deere thresher, he threw his clothes to the floor, the cool sensuality of the Armstrong tiles causing insensate emotions on the broad, excitable areas of his bare soles. He was in a shimmering mist, nothing mattering but the pitiless defoliation of this adorable hellcat who had brought her soiled body to mark their reunion. His cruel, sensual lips parted, the liberated teeth laughed with barbaric glee and sank into her neck.

"Oh, Iz! Iz!"

Her own teeth were busy beavers hewing a scarlet path on his shoulder, reopening many of the wounds he had suffered in the field. Breasts swollen to aching mounds of desire crushed his chest; her thighs, taut, supple, greedy, pressing his, hothouse hands searching, finding the wellspring of life and love and godhead and it was springing —and well. Her tongue tip was a mine sapper roaming his ears, gums and throat for buried caches of erogeneity; his long, tapering fingers responded, kneading, cosseting the holy labyrinths causing tactile sensations of indescribable karma, dharma and pepitone.

From that Norman Hekler-designed kitchen radiated the unstoppable impulses of their incendiary liaison to the alarmed sensors of an unprepared world. Several stallions went berserk at a Cheyenne rodeo, bucking off their riders into the gravel. A seismograph at the University of California at Berkeley shuddered, registering an unbelievable 71.4 Richter which hurled the leadership of the Free Sex Movement into a Newman Club seminar on "The Shining Shield of Abstinence," then attacked an aroused Sperry Rand satellite tracker. In a cold-water flat on Greenwich Village's Morton Street an orgone box glowed with a white-hot heat that sent beads of perspiration rolling down its galvanized sides—and there was no one within. Through it all the song of sex roared unabated in the obsessed body of Israel Bond; sparkling glissandos intermingled with ernie durandos; fugues swelled into full-blown rizzutos, and her thighs were yielding to his, revealing concept

49

and cosmos, bread and wine, death and transfiguration, port and starboard, David and Lisa, night and day, day and night for she was the one and she was Earth Mother, releasing at last the boiling life-force in her depths, and he was taking it, reshaping it, selling it to Goodwill Industries, for he was Earth Father and father knows best and he was in the clutch of a centrifugal force, surrendering to it and his head slipped down, down, down into a pool . . . sweet, dark . . . so sweet, so dark. . . .

9. Where Love Has Gone

She helped him pull his head out of the bowl of chocolate pudding on the kitchen table.

He had failed her.

"Well, how was it, Iz?" she said with ill-concealed bitterness.

"MY-T-FINE."

10. Tell Me, Where Can I Go?

Once again Israel Bond's rapier wit saved the day.

For ten minutes Liana Vine laughed her adorable hellcat head off. "Iz, what a stupendous pun you just made!"

He chucked her under the chin. How had he ever stayed away so long from this warm, bewitching, understanding girl? He would reward her patience for he knew that she must still be seething like a tidal wave which can find no coastal town to obliterate. The rapier would become the rapist!

Before he commenced his second onslaught he was struck by an inspiration. If laughter and love were so inescapably intertwined for Liana and him, why not combine the two? Poking about, he found an Allan Sherman album chock full of the chubby little fellow's devastating song parodies and placed it on the stereo that serviced the entire Vine manse with music.

So it was that, accompanied by Sherman's "gift of laughter," he took Liana Vine once more; this time it was no cold, furious exhibitionism, but mature and rich, a love of giving, not sadistic taking, and they melded soul-searing climaxes with guffaws at the comedian's rib-tickling punchlines. Fortune was with them, the funniest bits, "Sarah Jackman" and "Drapes of Roth," issuing from the speaker at the exact moments of fulfillment in their sexual congress.

Congress was in session a long, long time.

"Think you'll ever forget that third coal scuttle player now, my dearest angel?"

"Don't ever go away again, Iz. Stay. Marry me, live with me. I don't care which." Then she said, "Ouch!"

"Did I hurt you, *schoendeleh?*"

"No, dearest. I'm sitting on an ant button. But you haven't answered me."

"Hold on thar, Miss Liana. Thou has fain tempted me, fair damsel, but it can't be done that quickly. I'll have to ask out of Mother's, maybe help train another agent—uh, salesman, to fill my 10-D wing-tipped Florsheim cordovans."

Her hand flew up to her mouth. "Oh, my God! I meant to tell you. . . ."

"Meant to tell me what, my funny valentine who makes me smile with my heart?" He saw her strained face and his heart ceased smiling.

"Forgive me, Iz. The thought of seeing you again, doing this . . . it just drove everything else out of my brain. Iz, there's no need for you to go back and resign. You're out of a job."

He pulled himself up. His voice was harsh. "What the hell do you mean by that?"

"I heard it on the radio just before you came in. A bulletin from Tel-Aviv. Mother Margolies' Activated Old World Chicken Soup factory . . . it's been blown up!"

11. There's Something Strange In The Heir

London?

Israel's secret service handed what could be a knockout punch and Op Chief Beame was ordering him to London?

Beame had been quite dictatorial about it on the phone. "This is a Mem Echod, repeat, Mem Echod. Rendezvous with 113 at Point WCH, Station Benny der Graiser, for further instructions. Shalom."

"Are you in Foam Rubber Acres yourself, Op Chief? Zvi is—"

The line went dead.

He shook his head. Beame's off his—and despised himself for the cheap play on the name at a catastrophic time like this. Well, Beame *was* off his beam, damn it! 113 had been Zvi Gates' designation and lovable, laughable Zvi Gates was gone, buried in some Godforsaken spot in the green hell that was the El Tiparillan jungle, with only kindly Sister Sweetcakes, "The Swinging Nun," caring enough to stop by sometimes and place a portion boiled beef on his grave. No, Beame isn't the type to go off the deep like HaLavi. There's a logical explanation, idiot. A new 113. He felt a childish resentment toward the man already and cursed himself for being unjust.

Wait! Mem Echod!

Gottsedanken!

Mem is Hebrew for—M! Echod for—One! Mother was alive! Benny der Graiser was Yiddish, the *lingua frankel* of the truly cultured "in" of the world. Benny the Great, the Big, or Big Ben . . . London, his next stop.

Now HaLavi's new gear was in his bags and he was looking out the window of an El Al jet 31,000 feet up and he wanted a woman.

A strange symbiosis of sex and air travel caused a continual disquiet in the body of Israel Bond, dreamy local sensations caused by the hum of the engines, perhaps, or the clouds that suggested tremendous, fleecy mega-breasts. This merger of lust and altitude had grown more pronounced of late on his many jet excursions. (He would fly nothing but pure jets because of his Electra complex, a fear of turboprop

52

planes.) And it was becoming peripheral. Sometimes he would feel the stirrings in a cab on the way to the airport, other times while telephoning for airline reservations, and once even in a supermarket where he saw an item whose very name seemed to spell out the linkage—Airwick.

To quash the feeling he busied himself with *The New York Times*. There was a wrapup on the explosions, minus the one at Mother's which had broken too late to make the edition. The FBI had been ordered to investigate the 178 deaths at 4,000 disasters; dozens more were dead in South America and Europe. As Sahd Sakistan mourned King Hakmir, Grand Vizier Ben-Bella Barka had flown on a hush-hush mission to London. New York's Mayor Lindsay had been offered a plan for a new police review board which would review the decisions handed down by any civilian review board; the mayor had promised to review it. Andorra was on the verge of detonating its first H-bomb, but its nuclear researchers were hesitant about doing it on their own territory; not to set it off would mean loss of face since a belligerent Lichtenstein soon might have its own bomb; to set it off would mean saving of face but loss of Andorra.

"Coffee, tea or LSD!" chirped voluptuous Shoshanna Nirvana, the curvaceous, black-eyed Yemenite stewardess. "The latter," Bond requested, popping the cube into his sensual mouth; for three hours he was afloat in a reverie that enabled him to see music and hear Marcel Marceau's entire act. He came out of it as the pilot, Captain A. B. Nathan, announced the descent into London.

Point WCH was code for the William the Conqueror Hotel.

"Cabbie, take me to 1066 Hastings. Do it in less than ten minutes and there's a handful of farthingales, forepence and jujubes for you." On the way to Cheapside they passed what had been a delicatessen, its windows blown out; on the sidewalk lay salamis and tongues in the appalling rictus of death.

"Gar! Fifteenth bloomin' one I seen like that todye. Someone's got it in for the bloody Yids, they 'as." Bond cut four farthingales from the bigot's tip, kicked holes in the cab's rear tires with his heel knives.

He paced the room hour after hour, each new disaster aired by the telly deepening his concern. He looked at the two-foot mound of Raleigh stubs and berated himself for the habit. Maybe the coupons would cover the lung operation, he smirked. Swallowing 103 Luden's cough drops to alleviate a slight sore throat, he moved to the door when the rap sounded, opened it wide and was driven back by an agonizing blow to his tender stomach by the muzzle of a .44 Serenata-Holmes.

"Just put your hands behind your neck." The speaker was a sandy blond with a bandage on his forehead. He was slim, of medium height, wore a black Haly's M.O. windbreaker, khaki ducks and white hush-puppies. With his left hand he removed the outsized Italian wrap-around sunglasses that blocked off a third of his face.

"Neon! Neon Zion! You damn fool kid! Don't you remember the Matzohball caper?"*

"Stow it, mac. The quick brown fox jumped over the pickled lox."

A rage shook Bond. This damn snotty punk, an ex-Israeli Peace Corpsman who owes his life to me, is pulling guns and demanding countersigns as if I'm some runny-nosed recruit. There was no choice but to play along:

> *"Folks who live on Quemoy are known as Quemoyim,*
> *"And all these Quemoyim, for damn sure, are goyim."*

The breath whooshed out of the kid and Bond realized how nervous he must have been. "Thank God it's you, Oy Oy Seven! I had to do what I did. Orders."

"What the hell is bugging Lazar Beame? Doesn't he know who I am?"

Neon lit a Raleigh. "Mr. Bond, since it happened, nobody knows anything any more or trusts anybody. Sure, you look like the man I grew to worship on that terrible isle, but you could have been a TUSH-y† with a plastic surgery job." He closed his eyes. "Here's the scam: Somebody disguised as one of the tourists left some Calgonite, at least 200-zis' worth, in the front wing of M.'s factory. It went off at 5:30 P.M., just missing the departing tour group, and that was a break, at least. Imagine the stew we'd be in explaining five hundred American deaths to the State Department."

"They weren't really after the Yanks. We were the target."

Neon slammed his fist into his palm. "Yes, but how in hell did TUSH know the factory was a cover for M 33 and ⅓? Another thing . . . with the exception of Oy Oy Five, missing, presumed captured, and you, sir, all the Double Oys are dead. It's foolish to suppose TUSH hadn't heard of you. But how did they know who the others were?"

Bond bit his lip. He knew, but that could come later. "Who got it at the factory? How bad is M.?"

"Crippled. In a wheelchair. I was next to her when it happened. A hundred cases of Mother's Activated Old World Kosher Charcoal Briquettes fell on us. Got my head banged up, but that's all. Uh, you and Lilah were kinda close, I take it. . . ."

Bond sprang at Neon, dug his long, tapering fingers into the lad's shoulders. "Lilah! What about her?"

Tears streamed from 113's eyes. "She wasn't as lucky. It hurled her into the gefilte fish vat. It was boiling."

"The others?" He let go of Neon and stared into the London night. In his rage he whipped out the Chris-Keeler and fired through the window into Berkeley Square. The nightingale fell dead. "The others?"

---

* Described in *Matzohball*, I think, but maybe it was *Loxfinger*. Why take a chance? Buy both. In huge quantities.—S.W.

† An agent of TUSH.

THERE'S SOMETHING STRANGE IN THE HEIR

"Aide de Camp de Camp, gone . . . Section Psychiatrist Pippikel, gone . . . Mendel the Mantis, gone . . . a few dozen factory workers, too. . . ."

"HaLavi?" Was the little genius of weaponry out of it, too?

"He's O.K., sir, s-s-s-ort of. He had just stepped out for a breath of hot stale air—he can't stand air conditioners, you know—and he was knocked down. But he came out of it kinda funny. I was the first to get to him. He'd been hit a glancing blow on the head by a board with one of M's immortal proverbs painted on it, which said 'HELL HATH NO FURY LIKE A PLYMOUTH.' He looked at me and said, 'You know, Neon, if you keep feeding massive doses of iron to Persian lambs, you might very well get steel wool.' I didn't say anything to that, but then he said, 'Lord, if I don't do something quick they'll die!' And he pulled these shoetrees out of his lab coat and. . . ."

"Say it," Bond commanded.

"He took out these shoetrees and started to *water* them with a sprinkling can. Then Lavi got real worked up. He started to tell me about some theory of his. 'You know, Neon, if it is theoretically possible to engrave the constitution of Israel on the head of a pin is it not also possible for the entire *Knesset** to meet on it as well? In a land as small as ours space is a precious commodity. By moving the building onto the pin, or, perhaps, even all of Jerusalem. . . .' and that's where I called an Alarm Aleph and Op Chief Beame took him away."

Bond was pulling on his trenchcoat. "We're wasting time. Let's get the hell home." He swore to the mocking moon over the church spires: I'll get revenge for all of this. The insolent moon jibed back: *"I'm from Manakoora. You Gotta Show Me."*

Neon dragged on his Raleigh. "You're not going back, Oy Oy Seven. Mem Echod order. You've a job that starts right here in London town."

Up your foggy day, Bond grumbled to himself.

"And . . ." Neon moved to the door . . . "if I'm not mistaken it starts this second."

A bronzed, gaunt man in a double-breasted sharkskin suit with rakish fins protruding from the armpits entered. His face was distinctly Arabic, proud, barbaric, distinguished by a hooked nose. A yellow fez perched atop his grey locks. "Israel Bond, I am Ben-Bella Barka, Grand Vizier of Sahd Sakistan. Please come with me. Your duties commence at once."

"Goddamnit! What the hell is going on in M 33 and ⅓? Are they trading me to the Arabs for Suez and thirty oilfields?"

Neon smiled. "Something like it, sir. M. has consented to have you act as the Secret Service of Sahd Sakistan on a temporary basis. You are to guard King Hakmir's son who is in a ticklish spot, untested and surrounded by enemies. The new monarch was specific in requesting

* Israeli Parliament.

you. Ben-Bella Barka found him living here and contacted our P.M., who agreed to the deal."

"Deal?" Bond kicked the wall, dislodged three coats of Sherwin Williams and a cheap reproduction of a Kim Novak painting. "This is lunacy! The big show's going on in Israel; they're bumping off our Double Oys, crippling our Number One, and I get sent on some f—— tinhorn assignment! Listen, Ben-Ball Breaker or whatever your name is . . . what's in this for my country?"

The mouth was taut and cold. "A great deal, Mr. *Boor*. In return for guarding His Majesty, Sahd Sakistan, a believer in *realpolitik,* is going to be a force for your nation's welfare in the United Nations. Our alignment with you on key issues will lure the Asian states from their ties with the Arab bloc and perhaps even convince our Middle Eastern neighbors to end their unprofitable obduracy. There is more at stake for you in Sahd Sakistan than in Tel-Aviv, no matter how horrendous your present tragedy."

"He's right, Oy Oy Seven," Neon asserted and Bond knew it. "M. says I'm to be your assistant."

Bond's shoulders slumped. "Where is His Majesty?"

"He is having his fitting for the coronation. Come with me, gentlemen."

Ben-Bella Barka's block-long Rolls took them to an address in fashionable Mayfair and parked in front of a glittering salon on Darn Cat Mews. They got out and walked the block to the entrance. Several English shopgirls with delicate tea biscuit complexions tittered and blushed as the darkly handsome Israeli favored them with a cavity-free grin, an elegant bow and several sure-fingered probes. "His Majesty is in Monsieur Pierre's suite, gentlemen."

And in Monsieur Pierre's arms, it developed. The designer, clad in a purple toga and hunter's-green Jamaicas, held the tiny monarch to his heart. *"Mon roi, mon amour . . . je t'adore. . . ."*

Then a wild eye caught Bond's bemused face and a spidery hand pushed the Frenchman's face aside cavalierly. "Split, you disgusting Frog! Here's the real stuff in life to cling to—my sweet Super-Jew. . . ."

Sahd Sakistan's new monarch looked like the cat about to swallow the aviary. With a frenetic series of ballet leaps he vaulted to Bond and threw his fragile arms around his neck. "Oh, blessed spirit of Oscar Wilde, it's the beefcake bonanza, the Eldorado of erectility, the mother lode of musculature, and it's mine, mine, mine. . . ."

Bond had groaned as soon as he had been able to take a good look. His heart hit his heels as he recognized the elfin Negro with the Dick Van Dyke beard, horn-rimmed glasses and Courréges dress and white boots, who had been tapped by destiny to rule a nation.

Baldroi LeFagel!*

* Brother of Sister Sweetcakes, the "Swinging Nun." Buy *Matzohball,* Pocket Books, Inc., 1966, $1.

12. A Strong Man Weeps

"I will *not,* I will *not,* I will *not!* Let Israel be overrun by Egypt, let the sky fall in the sea, let banks fail in Yonkers. I will not!" Bond stormed.

Then his patriotism triumphed and he consented with utmost reluctance to take Neon's quite sensible advice.

"If you're going with His Majesty tonight to the night club, it ill behooves you to look out of place. He may already be shadowed by TUSH, Mr. Bond. You must not look as though you're guarding him. You must appear to any tag* as one of LeFagel's companions."

So Bond put on the dress.

After the first shock of seeing the smart Cecily of Sicily two-piece electric blue Jersey knit cling to his lithe, muscular frame, he found the freedom of the skirt somewhat refreshing. After all, Scotsmen wear these kilt things all the time, he reasoned, and certainly no one finds the Scotch unmanly. And the blonde wig . . . well, hadn't Harpo Marx worn one like it during his career? And Harpo had never been suspect. As for the shaped Cuban heels, doesn't José Greco—

Knock it off, Bond; stop the rationalizing.

You're afraid of what you're wearing, afraid you might like it.

Hadn't a renowned observer of mankind once said, "There's six percent of latent homosexuality in every man"? Who was it now? Freud? Jung? James M. Cain?

And, Mr. Bond, his inner self continued, what man taking a shower at the Y has not looked at the man in the next shower and said to himself: "That's another man taking a shower there"?

He thought: We all have hangups, hidden fears. I was in LeFagel's room a few minutes ago and he showed me a picture he'd taken of New York City's Chrysler Building with its gleaming needle top. He was positively misty when he looked at it. I know what it represents to him, of course. Looking at it from my standpoint, it made me feel sexually inadequate. And imagine a poor bastard who's hooked on junk . . . to him it must seem to be the mother of all fixes and he'd die happy if he had a 1,500-foot arm and a 200-foot-wide vein.

* An espionage term meaning one who is employed to "shadow," "tail" or "trail."

ON THE SECRET SERVICE

Snap out of it, Oy Oy Seven! The philosophical mood, not the dress. There's a job to be done for M., Eretz Israel and the ruler of Sahd Sakistan. You're on the secret service of His Majesty, the Queen.* Thank heaven Neon's working out all right. Smart young kid, even suggested he'd go on ahead and case the joint because we shouldn't be seen together.

Bond finished with the base makeup and Maybelline eye shadow. Not bad. I could never be one of those truly *beautiful* girls, but I'm undeniably . . . *interesting.* A touch of Tangee on my cruel, sensual lips and it's off to Soho with Baldroi LeFagel and an evening at King Baldroi's own nitery, the Gayboy Club.

LeFagel was a vision in crinoline and lace when Bond stopped by to fetch him. "I feel so Scarletty O'Hara tonight . . . magnolias by moonlight . . . warm winds whipping whatever part of the slaves Ol' Massa missed in the afternoon. . . ." He suddenly stared at Bond. . . . "Why, you've turned, you've turned! *O mirabile dick, too!* Glory, glory. . . ."

"Cool it, LeFagel. This is just a disguise. Don't get your hopes up."

LeFagel winked. "I'd much rather get *your* . . . hopes up, you bonny, brawny thing." He clasped his hands in a prayerful attitude.

Gottenu! Bond sighed. The double meanings start already!

As the cab rumbled through the night a blanket of fog lent a sinister touch to the city. Good-o, Bond thought. It'll be hard to be tagged in this pea souper. He felt his purse, heavy with the comforting weight of the metal object inside, hoping he would not need to use it.

"Say, LeFagel, what's with the Old-South-by-moonlight getup? A man who's written such violent anti-white power structure novels like *Up Your Blue Toilet, Mister Charlie* and *Burn, Whitey, Burn in the Fire Next Time* has no right to look like a 19th Century plantation owner's imperious daughter."

LeFagel put an orange-tipped Phyllis Morris between his lips. "Oh, I'm over that phase. Not that I'm unsympathetic to my people's problems, you understand, but if they haven't got enough sense to better themselves by inheriting Middle East kingdoms the hell with them. Anyway I'm much too involved these days with the real movement, Bondikins."

"Call me 'Bondikins' once more and I'll kick your tail."

"And I'll accept it gladly, as a prelude to better things, of course. The real movement is typified by *One* Magazine, the organ—you'll pardon the expression—of the most vigorous of all the ethnic groups— us."

"I've seen it. It takes One to know One."

"Touché! Well, they haven't gone quite far enough, so I've initiated a One World movement of which my Gayboy Club here is the opening gun. Next, Gayboy Magazine, our slick entertainment-jammed periodical which will feature our Gaymate of the month—and what a coup

* Possible title.

58

it would be if the first centerfold attraction was Hugh Hefner . . . naked!" The tiny ruler shivered at the very thought. "It'll also feature our own comic strip heroes, Fagman and Birdie. In our version they'll *both* be named Bruce. And if the Fagphone should ring, they'll just never answer it, that's all. Oh, it'll be the wildest thing in publishing, sweet Samson, highly departmentalized, too. Our dear senior citizens will have their own section called the Gay Nineties. There'll be contests on 'Why I Switched' in twenty-five words or less with grand prizes like wrestlers and truck drivers. Oh, we're here."

Bond felt a sharp pain aft as he guided LeFagel toward the lavender-blue Dilly Dilly door of the club and turned to see an evil grin on the ruddy cabman. By thunder, the man had pinched him! Only his Double Oy training constrained him from punching in the brute's face. Then Bond smiled. The man had pinched *him*, not LeFagel. No matter which scene I make, it's *me* they're after, and he felt somehow reassured and waved back at the driver.

Down winding steps they went, into a dimly lit cellar crowded with tiny circular tables, no bigger than hula hoops, around which were clustered little knots of Gayboy regulars, their lively faces illuminated by candles stuck into Clorox bottles. At a small bar a fierce-looking, mustachioed man smashed his hand in front of the bartender, spilling drinks onto the sawdust floor. "I can lick any man in the world!"

"Our champion, Dawn L. Sullivan," whispered LeFagel. "Superb, no?"

In a pinspot on a miniature stage was a heavily rouged, marceled blond sitting on a stool, his legs crossed. He wore a pink Linkletter Calypso shirt, the ends tied at his waist, and the tapered red-satin slacks so popular in this milieu, Transves-Tights. He was singing in a throaty German accent.

> *"When we crawled in bed one night last week,*
> *"I found we had the same physique.*
> *"You brought a strange kind of love to me."*

Sighs and moans ensued. "Willi, you're fantabulous!" cried a plump onlooker.

"She *is* chi, isn't she chi?" the admiring king said.

"Who is she?"

"I'll certainly find out." LeFagel exchanged a whispered conversation with the plump onlooker, then turned to Bond. "That's a new one I've never heard of. Willi Marlene from East Berlin. She asked my maître de if she could go on tonight. Far as I'm concerned, she can go on *any* night."

"Damn it, LeFagel! Enough with the *fakokteh* innuendoes already."

"Jealous, jealous, jealous. Admit it. Cat got your tongue? Lucky cat."

Bond paid him no mind. He was thinking. Willi had asked to perform, Willi from East Berlin. King Baldroi, we may be in trouble right off the bat.

As Willi did a medley of bittersweet songs obviously dear to his enrapt audience, "Blowing in the Wind," "My Nancy With the Laughing Face," "Mad About the Boy" and a slow, specialized rendition of "Stouthearted Men," Bond scanned the layout. On the wall back of their table was a gallery of photographs of world-famous celebrities. "Are they . . . uh . . . special, too?"

" 'Course, silly Semitic sweetness. The squares would die if they knew. See that one of the big-league ballplayer? He's a switch-hitter off the field, too. And the nuclear scientist? Right now he's working on something for us, the Gay-Bomb." LeFagel pointed a finger. "Like that mural?"

It depicted one of the heroic moments of antiquity, a homosexual holding off hordes of Mongols singlehanded to protect his Greek city-state, the immortal *Fellatio at the Bridge*.

Willi demonstrated his versatility with a collection of risqué stories which had the audience in titters (one of them with a rhyming punch-line, "faggot maggot," wasn't bad at all, Bond conceded, writing it down in his notebook) and ended his turn with a rousing yo-ho sea chanty whose lyrics fitted in harmoniously with the general theme of the Gayboy.

Throwing kisses to all, stopping to bestow special favors on a few, he made his way to LeFagel's table.

"Your gracious, gracious liege, heartbeat of Swishdom, defender of man's unalienable right to be alien," he purred and knelt to kiss the blushing king's hand.

As he genuflected, Willi Marlene's right hand slipped into the back pocket of his Transves-Tights, Bond's eyes on it all the way.

Bond's fingers were without prehensility, it seemed. He couldn't get the damn clasp to open, cursing himself for not having tried a few dry runs with the purse.

Willi's right hand came out with a curved *kris,* its wicked silhouette standing out in the candlelight.

Bond swung with all his power and smashed Willi across the throat as the dagger moved toward LeFagel's heart. Willi Marlene fell softly on his back, a broken rag doll.

LeFagel was screaming from the top of a chair now, hurling the Clorox bottles all over the club in his hysteria. One of the candles touched off the stage curtains and it flared into a sea of flames.

Bond stood looking down at Willi Marlene's body. How good it had all been before tonight, he thought. The glorious killings by Moshe Dyan rifle, the Tzimmes-88, the frozen Milky Way, the ten-ton Matzohball. Now I'm at the nadir of my career.

To look at it from a professional viewpoint, he *had* done his job, the weight of the gun inside crushing Willi Marlene's windpipe. For now, Baldroi LeFagel was safe.

But he couldn't keep the enormity of *how* he'd done it out of his head.

I have just killed a man by striking him with a purse.

He turned his face aside so that he could not be seen.

Israel Bond wept.

13. Gas, Meter Of A Traitor

LeFagel snapped him out of it.

"Mr. Bond! Mr. Bond! I'm on fire!"

So now it's *Mr.* Bond when you're up against it, eh, King Baldroi? He resisted an urge to cry, "Burn, baby, burn!" and pulled the screaming ruler from the table top, beating out the tongues of flame with his hands.

The wild fire LeFagel had set off by his outburst of irrationality was spreading like . . . well, wildfire. Not a bad line, either, Bond thought, and jotted it down as he hacked and wheezed on the smoke.

Bond put the tiny fellow on his torn, aching shoulder and barreled through the clawing, howling Gayboy customers to the street, the cool air a godsend to his scorched body.

Depositing LeFagel in a trashcan, he raced back into the inferno three times, snatching twelve more trapped customers, dumping them all on the sidewalk.

"Oy Oy Seven!" There was a bleat from one of the blackened faces in the third batch he'd taken up.

Neon!

"Are you okay, kid? And where the hell were you?"

"Backstage. I just came to a minute ago. You've saved my life again, Oy Oy Seven. I wish to hell I knew how to—"

"Forget it, boychikl. That's what Double Oys were made for. Why were you backstage?"

Neon choked for a minute. "Goddam smoke . . . it's damn near burned out my lungs. Got a cigarette?" Bond slipped him a Raleigh. "I told you I was going on ahead to snoop and I found something." He looked rueful. "Trouble is something found me, too. I'd spotted this Willi Marlene actor making up in the dressing room and I saw one of those symbols on his wrist."

"TUSH?"

"Well, sort off. Naked buttocks were being kicked all right, but by high heels."

Bond snapped his long, tapering fingers. "TUSH's special department for killer queers. He was in the Gayfia."

"Well, I guess he'd seen me in the mirror or something, because when I turned around I got coshed real good." He rubbed the back of his head. "Sorry, Oy Oy Seven. I loused up my first big job and he got away."

Bond gave the youngster a friendly jab to the mouth, which split it and sent three teeth flying into the gutter. "He's been taken care of, fella." Several of the Gayboy patrons ran screeching down the street. Bond grinned. "See them running. I guess that's what they really mean by drag racing."

"Oy, mommeleh!" Neon's eyes bulged out and he was in the grip of an uncontrollable fit of laughter. "Damn, that's funny! *Drag* racing!"

Hey, Bond thought, looking at young Neon with new respect. The kid's a *laugher!* Hell, he laughs more than Zvi Gates ever did. 'Course, I'm sorry for what happened to Zvi, but. . . .

Back at the William the Conqueror he called for a parley.

"We've got to get the hell out of here. TUSH has a boatload of agents in London. But we'll throw 'em a curve. Instead of Sahd Sakistan, our next stop'll be Israel."

"I suppose I should thank you for saving my royal life, Bond-erooney," said a subdued Baldroi LeFagel. "It was precious of you. Mayn't I reward you in my own sweet way?" His eyes burned into the secret agent's.

"Yes, by acting like a king. Now go pack."

"Take this, Mr. Bond. It's a special edition of my new book of verse, *We Should Think About Spoons and Other Poems*. Bysie for a whilsie, luscious long, lean Litvak of my heart."

LeFagel flounced out and Bond signaled for Neon to follow him. He opened the fragile, scented volume whose text was printed upon cerise Scot Tissue. He read the title poem.

> *"We should think about spoons,*
> *"On haunted parapets kissed by beaks of owls.*
> *"Spoons, spoons, silver thighs of hate-love,*
> *"I pressed his thighs with molten spoons,*
> *"He slid down the mountain on his giderum.*
> *"Too short the peacock's sugared toes,*
> *"Too short, one long, dit-dit-dot, dit-dit-dot."*

Bond's cruel, darkly handsome face was filled with sorrow. The little bastard has talent, by thunder! He reread the line about "the peacock's sugared toes." Real talent, sensitive imagery. And LeFagel squanders it on this awful sexual aberration. Why, with a little toning down and some strict discipline Baldroi could very well be doing verses someday for Hallmark Cards. Sure, some of those ivory tower chaps might look down their noses at Hallmark Cards, but, by God, when you got a Hallmark Card you knew where you stood! He vowed: I'll straighten out this pint-sized pansy, make a real *mensch** out of him yet!

As he did his own packing he looked with regret on the electric blue Jersey knit dress that had served him so well on this grim night. Seems a shame to throw it down the incinerator, he thought. I'll take it along. There might come a day when I'm just bugged by everything else in my wardrobe and. . . .

Ben-Bella Barka's chauffeur took them to the airport, Bond keeping a rear window watch for any tailing cars, his hand clamped around the purse.

At the airport he bought them all insurance, including the new policy that covers death by plane crash in the waters of a holy shrine—sold only by Lourdes of London—and settled back to do some hard thinking as Neon and Baldroi snoozed. The London *Times* had more explosions to report, a total of 4,999 on the three continents. The Pinochle Royale would have made it an even 5,000, he reasoned, adding 4,999 and 1 and coming up with the inescapable answer.

The *Times* noted that in every instance but five the bombings had destroyed edifices which had some relationship to food and drink. The exceptions were five Halifax-to-New York freighters. Were these just random, unrelated incidents? Or part of the TUSH plot in some unrecognizable way?

James Bund's oblique references came back to him. "Operation Alienation." "Dr. Holzknicht." He'd have to tell M. and Beame immediately. Then a great guilt pervaded him. He'd also have to tell them that he had covered up the sordid betrayal of Eretz Israel by weaselly Nochum Spector, the little man with the big dream of world domination in the Matzohball caper.† Nochum had been M.'s nephew; Bond had not wished to hurt the old woman. But his silence had cost Israel almost 60 dead, including his buddies, the Double Oys. That part of the story intrigued him the most, the blown-up cab in Jerusalem after they'd gone to renew their licenses to kill.

It was obvious. Someone in the license bureau had fingered them in some way.

He would pay that bureau a friendly little visit.

Two cartons of Raleighs later, the El Al jet circled Lod Airport and angled downward. It touched the soil of Eretz Israel and tears rolled down his cheeks. He whispered:

"This land is mine. God gave this land to me."

The unloading took a bit longer than he'd bargained for. His personal effects occupied just twelve suitcases, but there were 86 others stuffed

* Man.
† In the Matzohball caper; *Matzohball*, 1966, $1.

ON THE SECRET SERVICE

with Raleigh coupons to get through customs. Enough for a medium tank, if M. bargained right, to help keep Israel free!

Lazar Beame was waiting in the Simcha, the ugly but gutsy little car produced in Beersheva by a French-Israeli cooperative. Beame was a short, stocky man of 55, with a tanned, stoical face. He was an ex-Double Oy himself who had moved up when he reached field-combat retirement age of 45. He'd begged for a two-year extension, but M. had turned him down: "You don't know what the really good wines are any more, your thickened waistline makes you unattractive to women and your golf game is way off. Worst of all, you can't work that hair-across-the-doorway trick any more. You're bald. Come in out of the cold, Lazar."

Beame's teeth were serrating a White Owl. "We're in Emergency Site Zaddik-Iyan-Gimmel-Gimmel-Yood ever since. . . ." He bit through the cigar in his anger.

Z-I-G-G-Y. Ziggy's! The popular Kosher restaurant on Jerusalem's Bezalel Street. Was that the new cover? Was fat, wisecracking Ziggy Gershenfeld, the Max Asnas-Toots Shor-Duke Ziebert of Israel, a big cog in the Secret Service?

"Surprised?" Beame said sotto voce so that King Baldroi and Neon, seated in the rear, could not hear. "I can hear your brain clicking. Yes, it's Ziggy's and, yes, he's way up in M 33 and ⅓; has been for years. There are some things you never learn until you get up to my level, Oy Oy Seven. Actually the Kosher restaurant front is fine for M. She'll be hidden away in the kitchen and besides it gives her a chance to cook while she's planning counter-operations."

They motored through the Judean hills, harsh and beautiful. Somewhere along the line three of the Simcha's four tires fell off, but the doughty auto chugged along with spirit. "These little babies can really take it, Bond," said Beame. The rear end dropped off at Jaffa Road and Bezalel Street, the motor fifty yards from Ziggy's, yet the sturdy frame made it right up to the door.

From the restaurant he could spot the Old City, which lay in Jordanian territory, and the words of an old Israeli spiritual rang in his head:

> "Ah looked ovah Jo'dan and what did Ah see?
> "Comin' fer to carry me home. . . .
> "A band of Arabs was a-shootin' straight at me
> "Comin' fer to carry me home. . . ."

They were hustled through the service entrance, down a hallway rampant with odors of pickles and stuffed cabbage De Vries, into the kitchen.

There was M.

She sat in a wheelchair, her slight legs made tree-trunk thick by yards of bandages. There were bruises on her forehead and cheeks and a plaster sticker on the tip of her nose. But her eyes had lost none of their keenness.

64

"Shalom, Oy Oy Seven, 113, and honored guest, King Baldroi."

After a round of salutations, M. suggested that Neon take King Baldroi to the front for a bite and seemed bewildered by the little ruler's arch response.

"The King has a bizarre sense of humor," Bond said, apologizing. He then unloaded his terrible secret from a heart that was bent into accordion folds by it.

Beame's reaction was instantaneous. "You stupid bastard! Nobody's feelings should ever be spared in this game. There's a ton of blood on your head, Mr. Bond. If I were you, M., I'd take away his number and throw him to the wolves."

M.'s answer took a long time in coming. "Op Chief Beame is correct, Oy Oy Seven. You have done a terrible thing." Bond bit his elbow in shame. "And a noble thing. I must be condemnatory in my official capacity, grateful for your concern in my human one. I disagree with Op Chief Beame's solution, however. It is unrealistic. Oy Oy Seven is perhaps our last hope, Mr. Beame. He will finish this assignment at least, before any departmental inquiry is held. The king still must be protected and this TUSH junta smashed. Maybe God will again strengthen Israel Bond's hand so he can redeem himself. Now, Mr. Bond, a detailed report on your experiences in Trenton and London, and your theories."

So that's it, Bond thought. This is my swan song. The folds in his heart gave way at the seams and the whole mess collapsed into his stomach. Popping ten Rolaids into his mouth to neutralize it, he recounted in an unemotional manner the whole story.

M. and Beame registered shock at his mention of Dr. Holzknicht.

The former pressed the pilot light button on the stove and in five seconds Ziggy Gershenfeld waddled into the kitchen, wiping his hands on his apron. "I heard Oy Oy Seven's report on these—" His forefingers touched his hearing aids. "I was wondering when you'd call me in." He was a round little man with bright eyes in a face that was a dead ringer for Harry Golden's. "If Holzknicht authored this thing it's something dark and deep. Certainly gives me food for thought."

"How odd, Z.," said M. with a nervous smile. "That very phrase 'food for thought' went through my mind when I first heard about it."

"Invert it! Invert it!" Bond was screaming.

"What the hell do you mean?" thundered Beame.

"Think about food! Think about food! Can't you see it?" Then Bond spoke slowly, as though recalling something from a dream. "Liana said it. 'We Jews still live in the kitchen.' She said it."

"Liana who? And what's it got to do with this whole. . . ." Beame started.

Z., Ziggy Gershenfeld, spread his arms. "Everything. She must be a smart cookie, your Liana. Now what ingredients have we got? TUSH . . . a sharp, perceptive psychiatrist iike Holzknicht . . . and he's great,

ON THE SECRET SERVICE

I got to say it about the *Deutsche momser* . . . the destruction of food and drink outlets . . . 'Operation Alienation' . . . your friend's knowledgeable observation about Jews and kitchens . . . there's a pattern in the whole thing."

Bond cut in. "Let's add some more elements. The preponderance of these disasters occurring in America's cities with big Jewish populations . . . others in South American and Western European cities also with big Jewish populations. . . ."

Z. twisted his apron in his hands. "I got to make some calls, lots of calls. I got a theory. I say we all meet here in three days."

Beame stuck out a belligerent jaw. "Can we wait three days, Z?"

"It's got to take at least that long to get hold of all the people I need to talk to."

M. nodded. "You shouldn't waste a moment then, Z. Oy Oy Seven, you'll keep an eye on LeFagel. Op Chief Beame, you'll give Z. any help he needs. For me there's a whole new factory to design. Someone give me a sliderule, pencil and some brown butcher paper. I'll start already."

Bond had Neon spirit LeFagel away via *sherut** to a Negev kibbutz, K'far K'farfel, where an old friend, Dr. Saul Rossien, was experimenting with the old chimpanzee-typewriters theory in comparative obscurity and safety. Some scientist had once claimed that if you set a thousand chimps before the same number of typewriters one of them might by accident duplicate some classic by Milton, Homer, Shakespeare, etc. So far the best thing Dr. Rossien had noticed was the work of one chimp who had laboriously pecked out: "One thousand chimps at one thousand typewriters."

For the next three days Bond moseyed around the license bureau, a shabby little office in the cellar of the Menasha Skulnik Building on Ben Yehuda Street. The office manager, Sharett Pincus, was one of those officious, small-fry bureaucrats who nursed his own little bailiwick jealously, but at the sight of Bond's hard face and gold security card he dissolved into a quivering mass of fear and cooperated to the fullest.

Besides Pincus, there were three others in the bureau, all clerks and all Jews who had fled from oppression in North Africa. They even looked a great deal alike—short, swarthy, with black moustaches. Pierre LaToole was from Morocco; Hassim Moonlight-Bey and Shofar Ben Blue refugees from Cairo. Naturally, their records were quite in order.

The sign was the first clue.

"Who authorized your bureau to put this up?" Bond said, his finger indicating a placard over one of the windows: LICENSES TO KILL.

Sharett Pincus stammered, "Mr. Bond, sir. There was a memo from the Ministry of Defense. I never ignore memos."

"Damn it, man! You should have ignored this one," Bond said.

* Hired taxicab.

Pincus paled. "I'll follow your policy and ignore all memos in the future, sir. But could you send me a memo on that?"

It was clear to Bond now. One of the three (he'd pretty well discounted Pincus) had forged a memo on MOD stationery, which was easy enough to obtain, dropped it in Pincus' box and the man had complied. There's no sense asking which one. They'll all deny it and two will be telling the truth, he thought.

Bond suddenly became jovial. "Sharett, you people do a lot of good work down here. My superiors would like to sort of express our appreciation. You and your good lads are invited to dinner at Ziggy's internationally famed restaurant tonight as my guests. It's all on the house." He slapped the man's back. "See you at eight."

Back in Ziggy's his face hardened again. "M., it goes like this: They knew from Nochum's tips who the Double Oys were, but they added an extra touch. They knew damn well that a Double Oy spotting a sign 'LICENSES TO KILL' would naturally walk to that window. The four Double Oys made the unfortunate mistake of going for renewal in a bunch. That was as sloppy a security mistake as mine was. So the plant in the bureau tipped off his bomber. When they all left the bureau in the same cab . . . sitting ducks."

M. sucked on a piece of rock candy. "How do you propose we smoke out the plant?"

"They've got some kind of food warfare mounted against us. Let's turn it on them. This is what I want."

At 3:30 P.M. Ziggy's was closed to the general public. A sign on the door said "Death in the Family."

M., despite her imprisonment in the wheelchair, was a dynamo in the kitchen. She knew just what Oy Oy Seven had in mind. "Lazar, put extra onions in the chicken soup, the hot Spanish kind. On the gefilte fish double the chrain;* no, triple it. Use the red cabbage around the meatballs, not the green. The pickles should be from the bottom of the barrel, the briniest ones you got. And throw some pepper on them; it wouldn't be such a crime. No margarine in the potato *kugel;*† it's not strong enough. Mix in a jar of my Activated Old World Chicken Fat from contented capons. Use the cream soda; it's got more bubbles than the root beer, and serve it warm."

At 8 P.M. Sharett Pincus and his three clerks walked into Ziggy's. They were greeted by Israel Bond in a brilliant silver dinner jacket with half-dollar-sized Tahitian pearls for buttons, an Arrow Gordon Dover Taper Glenn shirt with a Lash LaRue leather whip tie, Jantzen's black velvet evening swimtrunks, and Esquire Old Frontier bedsocks with the Norman Rockwell painting of Quantrell's Raiders wiping out a wagon train on the sides. Mr. Bond was charm personified on this gala occasion, a master of amusing badinage (his joke about a "faggot

* Horse radish.
† Pudding.

maggot" scoring resoundingly); in short, a hail fellow well met all the way.

And that glorious dinner!

"Mr. Moonlight-Bey, you've only eaten nine pieces of kugel! For shame! Little clerks with hollow legs need lots of nourishment. Come on, Mr. LaToole. Surely you can stand another pound of that gefilte fish! Mr. Ben Blue, open wide and nice; Mr. Bond'll give you another spoonful of relish. . . ."

Ninety minutes later the dinner was over. "Golly," said Bond, "I guess that was just about the niftiest meal I've ever had." He rubbed his tummy. "What do you lads feel about the dinner? Give me your honest opinion."

"Merci, Monsieur Bond. It was *formidable."* This from Pierre LaToole.

Shofar Ben Blue shook his head in disbelief. "Amazing. Amazing."

Bond lit a Raleigh. "Mr. Hassim Moonlight-Bey?"

Mr. Hassim Moonlight-Bey patted his own stomach. His full lips opened, revealing firm, strong teeth. From that mouth came a belch, no ordinary belch, but a mega-belch, one that sounded like the ten-second buzzer at Madison Square Garden combined with the horn on a 1931 Model A Ford.

Israel Bond smiled. Then he hurled his bowl of Mother's chicken soup into Mr. Moonlight-Bey's leathery visage with all his strength, squashing the aquiline nose to jelly. He dove like an avenging falcon on a lynx that has raided its nest, pinning the man to the floor and driving his fist against the man's solar plexus.

He stood up. Beame and Z. came out of the kitchen wheeling M.

"There's your goddam spy. Your gassy belch, Mr. Moonlight-Bey, so traditionally the Arab mode of expressing satisfaction with a meal, gave you away. Sweat him, Op Chief Beame, sweat him good so he'll talk. From this point on we're back in the old ball game!"

14. Call To Greatness

Z.'s three days were up.

What was left of the battered Secret Service of Eretz Israel looked with hopeful eyes upon the restaurateur as he shuffled his notes.

Op Chief Beame made the introduction.

"The Arab had some interesting things to say, but they can wait until Z. is through."

Z., obviously nervous, put down his notes, walked over to M. and began shuffling her notes. Bond, with one of his gallant, uncalled-for gestures, sprang to the table and brought M. Z.'s notes to shuffle.

Neon Zion, a 113 and unauthorized to take or shuffle notes at top-secret meetings, took out a deck of cards and was about to shuffle them when he caught Beame's stern eye.

Z.'s opening statement of his peroration was blunt:

"TUSH is trying to alienate the Jews of the Western world from Israel by destroying the one element it thinks is holding that relationship together—Jewish food."

Beame, who had been shuffling Neon's cards, glanced up at Z., swirled his forefinger in a circle around his ear.

"I am not crazy," Z. said with no rancor. "Dr. Holzknicht was the key to the puzzle, of course. During the last three days I have been in contact with those who knew him at the Schisselzelmknist Institute and they concede he is warped but a genius. As an illustration of that genius let me say that in 1955 he performed an unauthorized operation upon Gerda Sem-Heidt at the Konigsborgen Clinic. It was too delicate an operation for him to do alone so he enlisted the aid of two Rosicrucian chiropractors. One of them talked to me. Holzknicht gave her an external plastic heart and it works."

There were gasps from all but M., who made a notation on Z.'s notes, then handed them to Beame for further shuffling.

"The good doctor has made a thorough study of Jewish life, according to one of his old colleagues, and, I'm sorry to say, is more familiar with the milieu than most Jews. Undoubtedly, because he speaks our languages, Hebrew and Yiddish, he has been among us in disguise for many years in many places. He has noticed the shameful indifference of huge numbers of Jews toward Jewishness in recent years, which has been manifested in many ways: the rising rate of intermarriage, divorce and alcoholism, the slackening of synagogue attendance, dwindling affiliations with Jewish organizations, the weakening of respect between children and parents, the burning rush to change names, bob noses—this trend has been arrested for the moment by Barbra Streisand's celebrity, but it may surge again.

"He saw a phenomenon so common to us that we wouldn't give it a second thought. Have you ever noticed how Jewish we become, even the most disaffected of us, when we sit down to bagels and lox, corned beef, pastrami, kishke, borscht with sour cream, M.'s insuperable chicken soup, Manischewitz Wine, sour pickles, et al? In a twinkling of a boiled potato's eye that vestige of the emotional side of our heritage pops up. With each bite of the schmaltz herring we become ghetto philosophers; each bar of cream cheese sings the score of *Fiddler on the Roof;* each piece of rye bread—and suddenly we're fighting for the varnished heel with the union label again—makes us hum 'bum-bai-biddy-biddy-bum-bai!'; the sweet moments spent with the dear departed, the Mommas, Poppas, Zeydahs and Babas, are relived in a kitchen of long ago, and you now can appreciate the wisdom of Mr. Bond's lady friend, and, in short, we feel Jewish, and . . . and this is important . . . *charitable* to other Jews, to Israel.

"This is why Dr. Ernst Holzknicht destroyed the sources of food, many of the leading establishments where Jews congregate to eat it, and so forth."

Bond raised his hand. "I'd like to go to the bathroom, but tell me this. How does the bombing of the five Halifax-to-New York freighters fit in with your theory, Z?"

Z. laughed, "Schnook, you answered your own question and you don't know it. I'll help you. Where is Halifax?"

"In Nova Scotia." Israel Bond's face was flushed with shame. "I see. They were all carrying Nova Scotia lox."

"Vu den?* You see, just thinking about food has me talking Yiddish!"

Beame seemed half-convinced. "Let's assume everything you've said is true. But there's been no sign of any campaign against the Jews outside of North and South America and Western Europe. Don't they figure in?"

"No, because Holzknicht knows they don't count for a tinker's dam. You've got three and a half million Russian Jews who are in *drerd*† and they can't get out; you have a few more in the Arab countries isolated in medinas with no money, education or status; in the Far East you ain't got enough to buy a booklet of Hadassah raffle tickets. It's the Western Jews he's after. These are the ones who support Israel, don't you see? Remember, this thing is called 'Operation *Alienation.*' If the Jews of the West fail to buttress Israel in these crucial years when we should be growing we'll be so weak we won't be able to withstand attack . . . and all because some guy isn't getting his bagels and lox on Sunday mornings any more.

"Dr. Holzknicht knows it'll take years to rebuild the massive food structure TUSH's Calgonite planters have leveled these past few days. And by that time so many 'marginal' Jews will have left the fold that it would never be the same again anyway. For all we know, the damage is already done.

"I made some spot checks in every big city concerned. There's been a decline in these related activities already. The tourist bookings to Israel—down. UJA donations—down. Synagogue Sunday breakfast meetings—down."

M. turned to Beame. "Here, your trenchcoat is done. I'll shorten it later." She looked at Z. "Do we just sit on our hands? Is there no way to counterattack this monstrous thing?"

* What else?
† Hell . . . or Russia. The terms are interchangable.

"No, it's bad for the circulation. Yes, there is one chance. If we could get hold of any one of TUSH's big three, Auntie Sem-Heidt, Heinz Sem-Heidt or better still, Dr. Ernst Holzknicht, and make him confess this terrible scheme to the world, get the master plan, the list of all people paid for the bombings. With the proper exposure on TV, press and radio we could show the world what's happened and, incidentally, make our fellow Jews so mad they'll start going to daily services again and maybe buy some Israel Bonds, too. The question is: Who will shake these rats out of their nest and get the evidence?"

Operations Chief Lazar Beame answered him for all those present. He walked briskly to the bathroom, flung open the door and cried: "Israel Bond, come out and save Judaism!"

Bond slammed the door. "Now?"

"Yes, now!"

Bond emerged.

The grey eyes were cynical. "I thought I was just about all washed up with M 33 and ⅓."

"It's all changed." Beame was brusque. "Now I'll tell you all what the Arab said, from least important to most. One, Ziggy's was to be bombed. I intercepted the guy with a 100-zis charge. He's out of business for keeps."

Good-o! Bond thought.

"Two, he didn't know anything about the master plan; he's too small to be trusted with that info.

"Three, he does know where TUSH is located. The Sem-Heidts are operating a gambling casino as a front.

"Four, it's in the very place you're heading, Oy Oy Seven. Sahd Sakistan. So this is your chance to wipe the slate clean."

The slate? a peevish Bond thought.

"Go in there, Oy Oy Seven, smash that filthy cabal, get the documents, capture one of the big ones and make him talk, save the king from assassination, save Eretz Israel from disappearing into oblivion."

"Hold on, Op Chief. You're going too fast. I think I ought to make notes."

15. A Score In The Sky

It started its nerve-racking attack on his system the moment the Air India jet roared down the Lod airstrip . . . the old feeling.

Israel Bond, the most monumental task of his career awaiting him, lit a Raleigh and tried to stifle the libidinal monster inside clamoring for release by poring over the bulky report M., Z. and Beame had compiled for him.

"Sex Sexistan"—steady there, Oy Oy Seven; your eyes are playing tricks. Push this depravity from your mind. *"Sahd Sakistan"*—that's better—"is a territory about the size of Assault-Lorraine." *Alsace*-Lorraine, you pitiful, sex-haunted wretch!

It was then Miss Mookerjie, the olive-skinned, ebony-eyed hostess in the filmy red sari, a blue dot on her forehead, walked by his seat. "Can I be of service to you, Mr. Bond?" the sweet mouth spoke its polite singsong.

"I think not, Miss Mookerjie." Somehow his long, tapering fingers were closing around her willowy calf. He forced himself to read on.

"It has been playing both sides of the Cold War fence with adroitness. To illustrate, the Sahd Sakistani flag depicts a red, white and blue eagle clutching a hammer and sickle, beneath which is the motto, IN GOD WE TRUST—IF THERE IS ONE. Its principal exports are oil and malaria."

His hand was up to the butterscotch softness of the back of her knee, her scent of Lestoil spray causing his senses to reel.

He could stand it no longer, slamming the report to the floor. "Miss Mookerjie! Follow me quickly or I can't be responsible for my actions!" He clutched at his throat and stumbled into the alcove between first-class and tourist, where the stewardesses prepare food and drink. Once inside, he pulled the curtain shut and pointed to an I.D. bracelet on his right wrist. "Read . . . read. . . ." and fell gasping against the sink. Miss Mookerjie looked at the inscription on the bracelet, then into the tormented grey eyes, and smiled. "Of course, sir." Her nimble fingers flew to their appointed rounds and in five seconds her appointed rounds were revealed by the falling of the sari to her slender ankles.

With the unruffled efficiency of a trained servant of the air, she stripped Bond's Levi Strauss one-piece skydiver Score-Suit from his lithe, hard body and allowed a bronzed, muscular arm to draw her head against his chest.

"My name is Israel, O solicitous daughter of the Ganges," he said through cyanotic lips.

"Indira," she breathed. "Indira."

"Look, baby," he snapped. "I know *where*. I've done this before."

"No, Mr. Bond—Indira—it's my *name*."

Now they knew each other's names and that made it so real, so right, and his sensual lips, red once again, were sipping the bee nectar from hers. "Drink this." His command was hoarse, his body charged with expectation, as his hand bore a vial of desire-igniting Gallo Wine to her lips, setting her afire, and they began a fantastic flight pattern to fulfillment 150 miles an hour faster than the jet was going, making a mid-air adjustment to correct any weightlessness, and they collapsed onto a carpet of something green and cool, spent and content.

"What's this sticky green stuff, Taj Mahali dolly?" He prayed she would find favor with the sparklingly conceived internal rhyme.

"We are reposing upon the Royal gelatin which was to have been the dessert on this flight."

Two jetstreams of Raleigh smoke misted the window. "We made it on Royal gelatin, eh?" His grey eyes twinkled with levity. "I guess this is what they mean by a Royal—" but he aborted the witticism in an uncommon fit of good taste. He would not cheapen the moment this magnificent jewel of the East had granted him. "That blue dot on your forehead, Indira; it's gone."

She tasted his Raleigh. "Yes, I am a member of the Sylvania caste and that blue dot always disappears after I make love."

Back in his seat he was disgusted with himself for employing the old I.D. bracelet gambit. He held it up to the light. "I am afflicted with a rare phenomenon known as *sat-air-iasis* and must have sexual contact lest I go into convulsions that could prove fatal to me and possibly result in misfortune to the aircraft."

Bond pulled up the collar of his expensive yet tasteful Hill & Range tweed trenchcoat ("It's what today's teeners would call real 'boss tweed,' " his South Philadelphia tailor had assured him) and drew pleasure from the label's claim: THIS GARMENT, IF PERFECT, WOULD BE AN IRREGULAR.

King Baldroi, his eyes two malicious darts, leaned across the aisle. "I saw that little bit of hanky panky with the hostess, Bondy bitch. Come now; tell me. What did you two do in there? Did she force you to commit natural acts?"

"Knock it off, LeFagel!" He regretted the phrase. The little bastard would sure as hell twist them into his own frame of reference.

73

To his surprise, LeFagel did not, flipping a sheet of scrawled-upon yellow paper into Bond's lap.

Poetry.

> *"Tiger, tiger, burning bright,*
> *"In the darkness of the night,*
> *"You've made an incredibly stupid bungle,*
> *"You've set fire to the whole damn jungle."*

Good-o! LeFagel's showing a definite move away from the aridity of his homosexual orientation. Though I wish he wouldn't pet Neon's head quite so often. Well, I guess Rome wasn't built in a day. Although Levittown *was*.

When the jet dipped over the Gulf of Aden he saw the name U.S.S. *Jew* on the side of the mighty aircraft carrier whose decks were laden with neat rows of Chickenhawk jet fighter-bombers. Sound psychology, Bond admitted. America already had one called *Wasp*; the new boat would make a lot of swell folks feel a genuine rapport with the Great Society. But what was a carrier doing anchored off Sahd Sakistan?

He found out as he stood in the customs shed watching the MBG lowered by crane to the sandy soil. "Mr. Bond?" An inspector nudged his elbow. "You are wanted in the inner office."

Beckoning for Neon and LeFagel to follow, he walked through a passageway to a door, spitting upon it as his trained Double Oy eyes reported it was made from Cedars of Lebanon. When he felt the object dig into his back his mind clicked out Position 71—from the old manual he himself had authored for M 33 and ⅓ personnel, "Simultaneous Sex and Self-Defense"—and he fell to his knees with a slick, showy maneuver and whispered, "Don't shoot; I beg you, don't shoot."

The laugh held a note of admiration. "Okay, Oy Oy Seven. I see your reflexes haven't dulled one iota. On your feet."

That twangy New England accent! So redolent of B & M Baked Beans in dark brown jars; raucous gulls swooping out of a stormy sky to carry off stray Portuguese children; the Splendid Splinter, Ted Williams, at Fenway Park, taking two, then spitting to right. By thunder, it was. . . .

"Monroe Goshen! You old lobster lob! You Penabscot putz!" With delight he hugged the sawed-off man with the dour Puritanical visage whose slight frame was draped in a herring-scented Gloucester nor'-easter trenchcoat . . . Monroe Goshen, operations chief of the Central Intelligence Agency's Mid-East Section, who had spent with Bond in Eretz Israel those last spine-chilling hours of the Loxfinger caper.*

Pouting at the physical manifestation of fellowship, LeFagel said,

* *Loxfinger,* Pocket Books Inc., 1965, $1.

"Well, that about tells the story, you heartbreaking Hebrew! It's the *'fay* fags who turn you on, right, Whitey? The *partzehs* on *schwartzehs* aren't good enough for you."

Bond pushed the querulous monarch away. "Look, your highness. This man's an old fighting chum of mine. I suspect he's here for the same reason I am, to keep your hide intact, so drop the green-eyed monster bit."

Goshen introduced himself all around. "True, your highness. My men and I came here on a carrier, ostensibly as part of a goodwill tour, but we've definite orders from the Tall Texan to keep you on the throne. If Sahd Sakistan goes Commie, we could lose a billion barrels of oil a year. Let's continue this discussion at my embassy. You'll all be my guests for dinner. Don't worry, Mr. Bond; CIA agent Brown will deliver that razzle-dazzle car of yours to the palace."

When the customs inspector observed that Goshen's black Simulac limousine with the United States seal on its plates was well on the way to Baghs-Groove, the capital city, he picked up a telephone and dialed an unlisted number. He spoke for a minute, then quaked as the iron voice issued instructions. "Ja, mein lieber Gerda."

He walked to the spot where the Mercedes Ben Gurion had been deposited by the crew. "One moment, gentlemen. I must affix Mr. Bond's temporary Sahd Sakistani sticker to his license plate," which he did, with an exaggerated show of grunting diligence. As the left hand smoothed out the sticker, the right was touching the magnetized end of a metal cylinder to the underside of the Alcoa bumper.

It was a homing radio.

Wherever the MBG was going, so was a tiny sentinel from TUSH.

Two minutes later CIA Agent Brown, a towering Negro in a trim Ray Charles trenchcoat, stepped out of the office and was about to start up the MBG when he saw the red sedan pull into the parking lot. "1965 Togliatti," he told himself. "Let's look at the little old manual." He opened a pocket sized book titled "Oppo Autos" and read: "Togliattis are manufactured in the Communist-dominated Italian town of Fiore by the Roberto Scinto dynasty, known ultra-left sympathizers. It is no coincidence that Togliattis are always registered to members of SMERSH (a contraction of the Russian words 'Smert Shpionam'—'Death To Spies'), SAMBO, the newest top-secret surveillance cadre organized by a distrustful Moscow, whose initials stand for Smersh Also Must Be Observed, and TUSH. SMERSH and SAMBO invariably use Dagroes as drivers, opining that Swegroes, Spigroes and Bulgars are too dimwitted to manipulate the vehicle. The latter breeds, however, may accompany Dagroes as strong-arm men. TUSH, most imaginative of these clandestine networks, *will* use a Swegro as a driver if he has passed a driving test administered by a Dagro, mutation Bulgar or a Spigro with no less than 25 percent Dagro blood."

No doubt of it, Brown reckoned. The Togliatti is here to tag the

MBG. Might make things a bit sticky later on for Goshen's Israeli pal with the bigshot reputation. I'll have to see that Mr. Bond gets an edge on these scum!

"Hey, boys!" He called to the usual gang of ragtag Arab urchins pestering the deplaned tourists near the taxi stand for cigarettes. He waved a pack of Waterfords and they raced to his side. Brown spoke to them in Sakistani, distributed the cigarettes, and watched them as they sprinted to the Togliatti, sportively climbed over and around it until the swarthy, hatchet-faced driver, whose woolly poll, thick Negroid lips and Sicilian curses stamped him as an unmistakable Dagro, shooed them away.

When the red sedan started up and headed toward Baghs-Groove, Brown got into the MBG, turned on the ignition and heard the beep, beep, beep of the homer planted by one of the boys under the Togliatti's license plate.

Brown smiled. *We're ahead of the game now.*

Not knowing he'd merely evened it.

16. Dee Dee, Da, Da, Da, Da, Dee Dee

As Goshen's Simulac rumbled through dark, narrow streets there came from a lofty minaret the ululation of the muezzin and they saw the faithful prostrate themselves in the age-old tribute to Mecca, holiest of Islam's shrines, then heard a second cry from the chanter that held a definite note of annoyance.

Bond smiled. "I'll translate. He's crying, 'No! No! You schmucks! Mecca is *north, north!*"

"This, your highness, is the native quarter, the fabled Cissbah," Goshen broke in with the Fitzpatrick narration. "It's so named because—well, look for yourself." There were burros and their riders making their water, as all good beasts and men must, against a dank, moldy wall. "Your father, King Hakmir, was quite science-minded. Well aware of the traditional usage of that wall, he had his researchers cover it with a gigantic sheet of Testape to create a sort of instant health diagnosis. As you can see, the third rider on the right and the fourth burro on the left are incipient diabetics."

"Can't we get any more speed out of this, Mr. Goshen?" said edgy Neon. "We're going at a snail's pace."

Not quite, Bond thought. He'd been clocking a snail that had started all even with the Simulac on the Via of the Hairy Houris and was outpacing it by at least one-sixtieth of a kilo per nonnautical dunam. They began to pass mounds of rubble that contained entire families, the fathers puffing pipes, children diving in and out of the debris in merriment, mothers at the bottom of the piles with old-fashioned papyrus brooms sweeping them together.

"Your late father's public housing project, sire," Goshen pointed out. "Before he instituted it, the fellaheen* had no debris to call their own and slept in sewers, puddles, marshes, etc. See how happy they are now? Generosity was an integral part of Hakmir's nature. He often told our ambassador, 'I've made my pile; now let my poor unfortunate subjects make theirs.' "

From the look in LeFagel's eyes, Bond knew Sahd Sakistan's new ruler had been touched deeply. Good-o! Perhaps King Baldroi will yet be—

The first volley stitched its way across the Simulac's windscreen† and he hurled LeFagel face down upon the Du Pont 501 orange and black Cottage Club carpeting. From the front seat he heard Goshen moaning. "I'm hit, Oy Oy Seven. Save the king. . . ."

"Monroe!" Bond's muscular right arm lanced out, pulled the CIA op chief over the seat and deposited him next to the sobbing LeFagel. "It's an ambush, Neon. Right in this narrow alley and we're caught like rats in a trap."

"Say, Oy Oy Seven, that's a sharp simile you just came up with, that rats-in-a-trap business. That one of your originals?"

"You bet, Neon," Bond told the worshipping 113. Maybe I'm off base lying to the kid, he thought, but what the hell—Neon's under enemy fire right now and it's no time to start shattering the kind of illusions that make men happy to fight, to die, if need be. "How's Goshen?"

"Shoulder wound. Not too bad. Who's the 'oppo' out there?"

Bond shouted over the next barrage. "About fifty Kurds in black burnooses blocking the alley. We're in for it, I'm afraid."

Bond could hear the twanging of Neon's crossbow and from the occasional screams at the end of the alley he knew the kid was giving a good account of himself. Time to start doing the same, Oy Oy Seven, he chided himself. He worked the back door open and dove into one of the piles of debris, the impact sending stones cascading down its sides. The patriarch at the top of the mound hurled a deep-throated insult at him: "Home wrecker!"

His long, tapering fingers slid inside his Neiman-Marcus shoulder

* Peasants.

† Britishism for windshield. Thrown in to give this book a touch of class, which it needs.

holster and liberated the ice-cold Colt 45. He yanked off its pop top and let the bracing malt liquor run down his parched throat. An excellent beverage, he knew, but no substitute for the weapon I need at this vital moment.

When he heard it he thought: I'm losing my mind. I'm lying next to a shot-up limousine in a fetid alley, slugs whistling by my dark, cruelly handsome face, and I hear music! And it's so familiar. *Dee dee, da, da, da, da, dee dee.* Yes, the first eight notes of the main theme from the motion picture *Lawrence of Arabia.*

The music swelled, came closer and the shooting ceased. He could hear utterances of awe from the band of attackers: "She comes! She comes!"

Bond got up and looked down the alley, blocked no longer by the Kurds, who had opened a pathway and were kneeling along its sides. Through it bobbed a woman on a white camel from whose neck hung a black box whence emanated the music—a tape recorder, he guessed. She wore a gold robe whose effulgence was doubled by the Arabian sun. A red tarboosh with a golden flyswatter for a tassel sat upon her head. Only two glowing coals, a pair of indescribably piercing eyes, could be seen over the top of her black veil.

When the white camel snorted, a cool, mellifluous British voice calmed it. "Be still, Latakia. Thy mistress commands it." The dromedary obeyed.

Those wondrous eyes swept over the grim faces of the Kurds, who held their smoking Bunning slider-carbines in their gnarled, sun-blackened hands, the pained expression on the wounded Goshen, the wide-eyed Neon Zion, the trembling, lip-biting elfin king, and then found Bond's unflinching grey eyes. For 120 seconds black eyes and grey eyes locked in a duel; then Bond's cruel sensual lips parted in an arrogant grin of desire and he knew somehow that under the veil her own lips were framed in an answering smile.

"Welcome to Sahd Sakistan, your Highness." There was respect in the voice, but no submissiveness. "I was a friend of your late, beloved father, King Hakmir, and have sworn to uphold his successor. Why these misguided tribesmen have dared to fire upon their rightful ruler is a mystery I shall endeavor to unravel."

LeFagel's composure returned. "We owe our lives to you, gracious lady. Who are you?"

A white-gloved hand reached under the camel's neck, touched a button and the *dee dee, da, da, da, da, dee dee* strain issued forth again. "You will always know I am here to protect you, sire, whene'er you hear the opening eight notes of my traveling theme music. I am Sarah Lawrence of Arabia."

17. Let's Do The Tryst

As the mystery rider interrogated the Kurds, Bond promised the pale CIA Mid-East Op Chief, "This'll stop the bleeding," and he unscrewed his belt buckle to remove a tube, squirting its contents on the hole in Goshen's left shoulder. "It's cherry salve. My mom used to *schmear* it on every wound we kids ever had . . . burns, knife slashes, boils, even a deep puncture I received once when I fell from a window and was impaled on a rusty fence post." Directly did he apply it the cherry salve drew the bullet from the flesh with a loud pop and the ragged edges began to knit. In a few seconds every trace of the wound disappeared, including an adjacent vaccination mark and a tattoo, I'M A BILLY FIELDS FAN.

"You missed your calling, Mr. Bond," the mystery woman remarked. "Those long, tapering fingers should be healing men, not ending their lives with karate blows."

Bond, placing Goshen in the rear of the Simulac, said, "You seem to know all about me, Miss Lawrence, which gives you an advantage, since I know nothing about you." The grey eyes challenged hers again. "And I'd like to—very much."

"Mount Latakia and ride with me, Mr. Bond, and we can discourse as I guide your auto out of the Cissbah."

Ordering Neon to take the wheel, Bond accepted a white-gloved hand and with the fluidity of the high hurdler sprang onto the veiled beauty's mount.

The cool, musical voice was deferential. "You seem to be no stranger to a hump, Mr. Bond."

"That expertise, Miss Lawrence, is something I hope you'll have complete knowledge of someday," he sallied, and drew an appreciative chuckle from her.

"You have a rapier wit to match that lithe, muscular body, Mr. Bond." She touched Latakia's ear and whispered, "Onward, noble ship of the desert." Latakia moved forward with an undulating motion that lulled them both into a state of euphoria. As they rode, Bond encircled her waist, his fingertips tingling with a strange sensation never before known to him. *Gottenu!* he thought, now it's happening on *camels!*

"I am a twenty-fourth cousin by marriage of the famed Lawrence who changed the face of Mid-East history," she said in her clipped, precise British manner. "As a little girl on our ancestral estate, 'Guanay's End,' which is situated in the center of the triangle formed by Saxonshire, Normanshire and Brokenshire, I was regaled by Pater's tales of my cousin's exploits in Arabia and vowed to make a pilgrimage to the area one day to retrace his glorious footsteps. A child's silly longing, I suppose, and I more or less had forgotten it because of the multifarious activities afforded members of my class. Pater was an M.P. for the constituencies of Sussex, Wessex and Essex and—"

"Perhaps," Bond interjected, "you'd be interested in the benefits of a locale very dear to me, My Sex?"

"Capital, Mr. Bond! You *are* an amusing chap! To continue: As the daughter of landed gentry I went through the usual rounds, riding to the hunt with my trained pointers, Alpo and Thrivo, humdrum semesters at the exclusive Miss Fenton's School for the Bored, where I majored in ballet, fencing, art and class hatred. There was never a shortage of dashing swains for the beautiful, accomplished daughter of an M.P., Mr. Bond, and I was constantly turning down marriage proposals from such eligibles as Ronald Duckblind, Brenfleck Coddingfeather, even Britain's most sought-after young gallant, Sir Marvin of Throneberry. Despite the flattering attention I sensed the innate emptiness of this decaying way of life. My ennui did not escape the shrewd eyes of Rector Justin-Tyme Mother, spiritual leader of our Anglican parish. Father Mother, when he heard the dreams of an impressionable girl, said, 'Then go to the Middle East and take up the tasks left undone by Lawrence of Arabia.' However, there was much to be learned before I could come here—the art of riding a camel, for instance, which I mastered after many months of practice riding on a carousel in Blackpool. England's most renowned armorer, Major Roothboyd, taught me to handle rifles, side arms and medium-range rockets; I was schooled in the many dialects of Arabic by Ibn Tard, dean of the Institute of Middle East Languages and Intrigues; dressed for the desert by Muslim D'Ior and taught to exist on a mere handful of tanna leaves a day. I came to Sahd Sakistan a year ago and introduced myself to Hakmir and the leaders of the Kurds and Wheys, meeting first with rejection, until I had the presence of mind to play my theme song. Having seen the picture, they were convinced I was, indeed, Lawrence's kin. It was this hard-won admiration, Mr. Bond, that made the Kurds halt their attempt to assassinate King Baldroi back in the alley. The Kurdish chieftain told me he had received a report that LeFagel was an impostor, a false pretender to the throne, and that a *real* pretender to the throne was about to arrive in Baghs-Groove."

"This smacks of TUSH handiwork all the way, Miss Lawrence,"

Bond said. In the next few minutes he gave her a recap of his adventures, including the showdown with James Bund, detailed descriptions of the episodes with Liana Vine and Indira Mookerjie, and threw in for good measure the Loxfinger and Matzohball cases, plus his entire sexual history.

As she stirred in his arms during certain portions of the narrative, he thought, Good-o! She's all worked up. Before long this captivating creature will be mine evermore. What a find! Beauty, warmth, a "class broad" from Great Britain with a tony upbringing. She's the only woman worthy of your love, name, number and license to kill, Oy Oy Seven. A man needs to sink roots some time, and maybe I'm too far over the hill to stay in this racket any longer—I've already caused the deaths of almost five dozen good folks. This magnificent woman in my arms can redeem me, uplift me and maybe, since it's obvious she's loaded, set me up in my own high class shoe salon (nothing but I. Miller's and British Walkers) on Kings Highway in Brooklyn. True, I've sworn to my sainted mother that I'll never place a wedding band on any finger except that of a Daughter of Sharon; yet, that too can be worked out. I know the moment I take Sarah Lawrence of Arabia in a way she's never known before, she'll see the ultimate value of Judaism and convert with celerity. Wonder if Milton'll give me a 25 percent discount on the wedding at the Pinochle Royale? He should, really—I'm his brother, and besides I saved the joint for him and I think I'd be justified in telling him so.

He was already under the traditional canopy with Sarah Lawrence of Arabia, the rabbi intoning the sacred marriage contract, when her scent nudged him back to Sahd Sakistan. "It's driving me wild, Miss Lawrence. What is it?"

"A special blend, 'Evening with Profumo,' made for me by Maitland of Moreland Street. I am pleased at its effect on your olfactory sense. But we are at the Road of the Feculent Figs and I shall take my leave."

He slid off Latakia and motioned for the car to halt. "Shall I see you again, Sarah Lawrence of Arabia? There are things a man and a maid must talk of and they are best said by moonlight."

For another 120 seconds black and grey eyes flashed fire and desire into two another, his crossfire causing the rim of her veil to smoulder, hers turning his Talon zipper into red-hot mesh, charring his Arrow briefs. "Some aim high for happiness, Mr. Bond, while others. . . ." She left her proverb unfinished, but its corollary proposition was quite clear.

"You haven't answered me, Miss Lawrence." His voice was husky, his hands betraying his febrile state by abrasive motions that expunged the lifelines from his palms.

"It is my wont to be each night at 9:30 at the Oasis of the Seven

Mentholated Consumptives to commune with the spirits of the desert. Good day, Mr. Bond."

"One thing more, Miss Lawrence. Learn Hebrew. You'll need it the rest of your life because, Miss Lawrence, from this moment on, it's you for me, babe . . . only two for tea, babe. . . ."

Was that a sigh breaking through the glacial British reserve? He was not to know. She issued a command and Latakia loped off into the distance, the sun transforming her into a golden figurine.

Well, Oy Oy Seven, he thought, she's named the trysting place. An oasis by moonlight—in the company of a heaven-sent woman. It can be the kind of cataclysmic joining of kindred souls to be found only in those Kathleen Winsor reprints you keep buying.

Gottenu! he breathed, and to somehow dispel the unendurable passion surging through his marrows, he swung his bronze, muscular arm and struck Neon Zion in the face, splitting open his startled subordinate's lips. "Someday, Neon, when you're a man of the world, you'll understand."

113 made no reply as he searched the haunted grey eyes of Oy Oy Seven for a clue to the outburst. There was none, save the curious word repeated over and over by the panting lips. "Moonlight . . . moonlight . . . moonlight. . . ."

18. Blood And Sand And Blood And Blood. . . .

"I have composed another verse," proclaimed LeFagel. Bond, hoping desperately for another artistic indication of a turnabout in the king's psychological makeup, squeezed his fists in expectation. The animalistic fury triggered by the dramatic eyeball-to-eyeball confrontation with the mystery rider had receded when the first puff of his Raleigh brought back the sordidness of the real world. Goshen drove on, immersed in some memory of his New England childhood, muttering, "Happiness is a harpoon in a white whale." Neon Zion, possessor of youth's happy resilience, was on his seventies in paddle ball, the puk-puk-puk of the ball furnishing a surrealistic punctuation to LeFagel's recitation.

BLOOD AND SAND AND BLOOD AND BLOOD....

On a ghostly night of yore,
A man tapped on my chamber door,
It was cold out, so I granted him a haven.
He said, "Kind sir, my name is Poe,
And I've been searching high and low,
Tell me please, sir, have you seen my f—— raven?

Good-o! Bond thought. Not a dot of deviation in that one. In an irrepressible gesture of goodwill he jabbed his potent left at LeFagel, drawing two fonts of claret from the ruler's mashed nose. LeFagel grasped the significance of the heart-felt demonstration and returned a shy smile that held no suggestion of effeminacy whatsoever. He seemed content to just sit, bask in the warmth of Bond's feeling, and bleed a great deal.

But the air of camaraderie flew away like a frightened sparrow when Bond, leaning out of the rear window, spotted the white edifice at the very end of the shoreline road. "Is that it?"

"Shivs." The CIA op chief made it sound like a four-letter obscenity. He saw the old deadly look on Bond, the smiling lust for battle that imparted a murderous glow to the grey eyes and the dark, cruelly handsome face.

I know what's on his mind, Goshen ruminated. He's thinking the enemy's in there, the ghoulish krauts who've killed and crippled his comrades, blown up his people's vittles . . . and my ol' fire-eatin' buddy's dying to go in there and have at them. But I spoke to M., Z. and Op Chief Beame via the carrier's Ship N' Shore Blue Denim Network and I know what the odds are of getting the goods on TUSH— maybe a million to one—and even Oy Oy Seven, the man I and the whole world have come to idolize, won't get out of there alive. I'm an atheist—the only day I take off all year is Madalyn Murray's birthday —but if I were the praying kind I'd offer one now for Eretz Israel, the Land of Palms and Pledges, and Secret Agent Israel Bond, the neatest guy I'll ever know.

They were cruising through the modern section of Baghs-Groove, flashing by a John's Bargain Store, Gino Marchetti's, a Little League Harem Boys Club, a movie theater advertising *Gidget Meets the Loved One* and *Crud, Son of Hud,* and then the Simulac swerved into a palm tree-lined driveway up to the entrance of the U.S. Embassy.

Waiting for them with a pasted-on smile was a weedy, sun-reddened man in a Benny Wasser orange Eden Roc-weave tropical suit and Redd Foxx safari beret, who introduced himself as Tender N. Callowfellow, the ambassador, with a promise of a dinner "fit for a—" he began to giggle—"king." So it was, the braised sloth paws in Bosco-flavored *eau de Conigliaro* parve fluoridated sauce a revelation to even the most jaded tastebuds, washed down with *vin scully* '24 from the vineyards of Chavez Ravine, and "of course, your Majesty, Ambassador Scotch—"

he chuckled again—"on the rocks," and he poured it over the dolomite chips.

"I think," said Ambassador Callowfellow, pulling a bell rope, "it's time for After-Dinner Mintz. Ah, there you are, Mintz, my man." A short, white-haired oldster entered and served them pungent circles of Certs on heated Pacific Plywood skewers.

Goshen and Bond spent the next hour discussing the job at hand, while Callowfellow and the king retired to the former's study for a chat about the upcoming coronation.

"I've splendid news," beamed Callowfellow, re-entering. "His Majesty has consented to have America host his coronation at the Sahd Sakistani embassy located in the Empire State Building in New York. It will serve to remind the world of the unbreakable link between our respective nations, and will have the benefit of our superior news coverage. I'm terribly excited about it."

"I, as well," retorted the bright-eyed monarch pressing the ambassador's hand in fond farewell, and then departing for his new home.

* * * *

Built by John McShain from a design based on a collect phone call from Norman Hekler, the palace of the late Hakmir was an up-to-date Alhambra of coral harrylimestone, with graceful Keds arches and stately Art Hoppe columns upon whose slanted roofs rested alternating cupolas and parabolas. In the front, lined on two sides by vivid purple rows of San Fernando Valley eggplants, was an immense pool on whose surface floated sprigs of wolfbane and spiderwort nibbled at by chattering les cranes, Great Northern Hotel auks, and a rare merv gryphon. Overhead winged a brilliant red herb jeffries flamingo like a flame in the sky, flying over the enclave to its lover nearby. Near the entrance was a pewter statue of the late monarch from whose nostrils came a continual spray of provocative Vegamato, the essence wafted to the Simulac's passengers by the thermal air current originating in New York's Wall Street known as the "Underwriters' Wind."

"Iz," said Goshen, "for heaven's sake, don't try anything foolish. As far as the world knows, Shivs is a perfectly respectable outfit that pays its taxes and keeps its nose clean. You can't go in there like Gang Busters without proof. Anyway, your first job's keeping his Majesty here safe and sound; we're all agreed on that. I'll be in touch. See you later, fella."

"Wouldn't think of it, Monroe, you ol' Rockport chowderhead," Bond pledged, throwing a salute to the departing CIA op chief. Once inside the royal suite, he told Neon, "Keep Tabs on Baldroi—or regular Coke, if you're not watching your calories," and was rewarded by 113's prolonged laughter. He showered with distilled Culligan rain water, applied No Sweat, the deodorant that checks unseemly perspiration by destroying the glands that produce it, to his virile armpits, removed his beard with the super-keen Schlock blade that gives a man twenty slick shaves and thirteen bloody ones, donned a heavy-duty Haitian Poppa Jacques-strap, a pair of Reginald Gardiner lace sunslax, an aerated Krishna Menon waistcoat of bleeding madras (LeFagel saw it, meowed, "I go for men who use Menon" and was cursed at by Bond for back-sliding), Royal Blakeman Andalusian bedsocks, slung on M.'s paisley shoulder holster with one of Lavi HaLavi's deadly new occupants inside, used flesh-toned Tuck Tape to strap the Instant Processed Cold Rolled Extra Strength Steel tool to his calf, put on the Korvette's luau car coat, and swallowed six Excedrins (there might be agonizing pain ahead) and twelve Benzedrine tablets (if there was to be pain, he wanted to stay awake and enjoy it to the fullest; it was, after all, as much a part of life as pleasure) and a homer radio capsule whose signal could be traced by any "friendly" with a standard M 33 and ⅓ Ribicoff-Javits bipartisan receiver-transmitter-juice blender, then inserted one of the new anti-homer capsules into his belt buckle compartment under the cherry salve.

"You're going on a job, Oy Oy Seven, against orders." A shocked Neon said it.

"Just forget what you've seen, kid," Bond snarled. "I'm going to take the MBG for a little spin. If I just happen to lose my way and it just happens to stop at Shivs, well. . . ."

To save time he slid down the copper rainspout outside the king's window to a rear courtyard and walked into the empty garage which once had quartered the thirty Cadillacs now sharing Hakmir's eternal rest. Grinning at him like an old chum was the grill of the MBG. She roared her delight at perilous adventures in the offing when he put her in reverse, depressed the accelerator, and zoomed out, the armor-plated rear deck killing the tethered sacred white elephant with a pulverizing smash to its side. He got out, clucked in sympathy, and pressed Button 5, whose concealed acetylene torch emerged. He used it to slice the tusks into portable sections, which he heaved into the back seat. Tough luck for Mr. Pachyderm, he thought, but what's done is done and there's a grand (or even more) piano in it for me.

As the exhaust from the MBG's quadruple pipes singed the Portland Cement driveway to the main road, the Togliatti that had been parked behind the garage for two hours eased out. The beep-beep-beep of the homer on the MBG made the four swarthy men exchange evil grins.

From 1000 feet up in a helicopter, the two cars seemed to the giant CIA Negro agent like insects, Bond's a silverfish, the TUSH vehicle a ladybug. The flapping of the huge sign being towed by the chopper was a disturbance Brown had long since gotten used to. It told the people below: YOU ARE ONLY 8126 MILES FROM FLORIDA'S FAMOUS STUCKEY'S, THE HOME OF DELICIOUS PECANS, SOUVENIRS AND PASSIONATE PAGAN LOVE RITES BETWEEN SEMINOLE INDIANS AND GIANT ALLIGATORS. A perfect cover, he knew; Stuckey's advertising was famous the world over and no one would question its presence in the Middle East.

Brown had been sitting by the chopper on the roof of the U.S. Embassy when he heard the gleep-gleep-gleep from the transistorized device in his pocket. It was one of the cleverest items ever created by the CIA weapons unit and would never arouse the suspicion of the "oppo" because it was not shaped like a cigar lighter, fountain pen, pillbox, et al. It looked like a radio. Goshen's orders had been succinct: "I've just left Bond at the palace to guard the king but he's got the smell of fire and brimstone on him, and I know damn well he's going to Shivs. Tag him by chopper."

Brown's binoculars caught the MBG shooting away at 87.9 kiloknots. Wow! Plenty of Gulden's in that engine!

When the hatchet-faced Dagro at the Togliatti's wheel heard the beep-beep-beep (picked up by the powerful antenna on the front fender and fed into the dashboard receiver) begin to fade he also increased his speed, sliding the syncro-dynaflush transmission into Forward Speed Six.

A Raleigh waggling in his sensual lips, Bond sped down the shore road eager for the hand-to-TUSH combat that could mean either life or death for his adopted country. Ahead lay Shivs, its sun-splashed windows twinking a brazen challenge: *We're here, Oy Oy Seven, the whole rotten Nazi bunch of us. Take us—if you can.*

Got to hand it to the krauts, he thought. For sure they've cleaned those windows with Windex and can see 100 miles in any direction—a pro touch all the way.

Engrossed in fantasies of revenge he did not pay proper attention to the fork in the road, berating himself as he saw he'd veered off the shoreline drive onto a bumpy spur whose route shunted the unwary driver into the hellish furnace of the desert.

"You stupid, albeit dark, cruelly handsome, bastard!" he railed at himself, but the self-deprecation faded from his lips when he saw the blinking red light on the power ashtray whose interior secreted his radio hookup. He pressed Button 175, the ashtray swiveled, hurling two dozen Raleigh butts into his lap, some still smoldering, but there was no time to grouse about petty discomfort, for the radio was in full view, a tiny vleep-vleep-vleep coming from the cantilevered coils.

Forget the "stupid," make that modifier "lucky," he grinned, kissing his reflection in the mirror. That right-hand turn had been providential. He had picked up a homer concealed on some car in the area. If he'd stayed on a straight course, he'd never have noticed it. And he blessed the slipshod, amateurish side of his nature that so often had stood him in good stead.

He gave the MBG's gas pedal the full weight of his right Andalusian bedsock and she escalated to 156.6, her extra-grip Firestone tyres*

---

* Manufactured in Great Britain.

more than a match for the sucking sand. With dismay he heard the vleep-vleep-vleep dying out and on a hunch made a 45-degree angle turn off the spur onto the desert itself, gunning her up to 176.2. There was a squashy sound; he looked back at the mangled burro and its nomadic rider splayed out under the merciless sun. His forefinger punched Button 200 and he saw the canteen of water and the medical handbook jet from the rear into the poor fellow's broken hands. Good-o! Beggar's got a 50-50 chance of survival now, he exulted.

Alarmed by the diminution of the MBG's homer the trailing Dagro two miles back also played a right-hand-turn hunch, a hideous smile splitting the hatchetface as the beep-beep-beep pulsed back.

Goshen's airborne tag shook his head with incredulity at the scene below, two high-powered chargers whipping up dust storms as they tore madly around and around in a three-mile-wide circle. It was clear now—the MBG also had been "homered," without his knowledge. Time to end it. He switched on the special channel used by the CIA and 33 and ⅓ to contact one another. The gents in the Togliatti might hear it too, but unless they had a Nicklaus scrambler, which was unlikely, they would get gibberish.

"Brown Shoes and White Bread to Rozhinkehs Mit Mandlen . . . Brown Shoes and White Bread to Rozhinkehs Mit Mandlen . . . come in please. . . ."

Bond understood the recognition signal at once and listened to the CIA tag's analysis of the dilemma on the ground. "Good-o! Brown Shoes and White Bread. Rozhinkehs Mit Mandlen acknowledges. Out."

He halted the MBG and clambered up the burning side of a powdery dune. He could see an arrow of dust streaking his way, estimated the Togliatti's arrival time at 90 seconds, 93 if its driver wore a Timex. From the shoulder holster he liberated HaLavi's scaled-down version of the Anna Sten gun, touched the eraser on his Ticonderoga pencil, which split the pencil into a tripod, and mounted the weapon on it with his left hand, sliding the cordovan Hickok belt out of the loops of his sunslax with the right. He reversed the belt. Its hidden side contained 100 notches, in each nestled a steel-jacketed denizen of death.

Better take a closer look, the CIA man thought, and he brought the chopper down 750 feet. Yup, the crazy bastard's spoiling for it, like Goshen said. Gonna take on four of 'em by himself. Guess he's everything he's cracked up to be. Better get down there and backstop him.

The glint of the sun on the MBG's silvery roof tipped off the Dagro in the pursuing Togliatti. He braked it 50 yards from the dune and the doors flew open, the four occupants diving into the sand. Bond, feeding the Hickok belt through the Anna Sten, opened up and heard screams from two of them. The Dagro grabbed at his chest and pitched forward on his face; a second, whose racial stock was unrecognizable for the moment, was also out of it, blood gushing from his forehead. He gave the remaining duo, without question Swegroes, a long burst. From the thumps he knew he'd put at least ten slugs in each. Not good enough, buddy boy, not good enough. It takes a damn sight more than ten slugs to stop a Swegro, he knew.

The Swegroes jabbered at each other for a second, then began a steady crawl toward the dune, leaving dreadful crimson trails on the white sand. He emptied the belt, certain he'd pierced Swegro flesh again from the howls of vexation. But they kept coming. And he was out of ammo!

From his vantage point he could see them dragging their riddled bodies inch by inch up the dune, their eyes malevolent jewels. "Don't come another step closer or you'll regret it!" Bond cried. "I was never inoculated for chicken pox."

Their answer was contemptuous laughter; they dug their octopuslike hands deeper into the white powder: "By yumpin' yiminy, we gwine cut you . . ."

They hit the top at the same time, their tentacles tripping Bond and sending him tumbling down the dune. His head struck the MBG's rear fender. It's all over, he thought bleakly as the Swegroes loomed over him, their faces widened by triumphant smiles. There was a flash of something metallic and the point of a knife bit through the luau car coat into the waistcoat.

Suddenly the Swegroes were upright no more. Both were on their knees clutching their guts, still yelling defiance. Five feet away stood a powerful Negro, his lips in a gelid grin, bluish smoke rising from the muzzle of a Lucky Thompson submachine gun. "Stay down, Mr. Bond!" The Thompson chattered again, planting 50 slugs in each Swegro, driving them to their backs. The smaller of the Swegroes looked up at the gunner in sorrow. "You could yust stop it. I tink I bane die now, baby." And the brown eyelids rolled over the blue pools.

The second shook a fist, continued to scream defiance and, back on his feet again, made a rhinolike charge at the CIA man, the steely fingers gouging into the man's throat. Bond could hear the newcomer's frantic grunts and he ignored the claret streaming down his side, pulled himself into a sitting position and snatched at a gun in the dead Swegro's hip holster. He put five bullets into the attacking Swegro's back, heard a groan and saw the man topple.

"You all right, buddy?" Bond said, then: "Watch it!" The CIA man spun to meet the Swegro's second charge, sidestepped it and retrieved the Thompson.

The Swegro turned, screamed, "Defiance! Defiance! Defiance!" took a round in the heart and lungs, clawed futilely at the CIA man, then muttered to himself, "Why should I do all the f——ing work?" and fell on his face again.

"Don't go near him," Bond shouted. He staggered to the MBG, took a fragmentation grenade from the glove compartment and waved his ally away. He pulled the pin and shot-putted it onto the Swegro.

A minute after the explosion, the CIA man sniffed at the remains.

"Well, there's a little fight left in him, but damn little, Mr. Bond. Let's make sure."

From the sleeve of his trench coat he wrested off a button and placed it in the Swegro's mouth. He folded his arms and waited.

"That's it. There was enough cyanide in that button to kill a hundred and forty thousand people, the population of Bremerhaven, Germany."

Then their eyes popped. The gutted mound that had been a Swegro stirred, and the mouth said, "The latest census puts Bremerhaven's population at a hundred and fifty thousand. Defiance! Defiance! Defi——" They heard a throat rattle. Then all was still.

There was no doubt now; the Swegro was dead.

19. Shivs, I'm Here!

Bond inhaled his 519th Raleigh of the day. "He was a tough one."

His rescuer nodded. "Swegroes usually are. Frankly I don't know why the other one copped out so easy. Let's give a look." He gave the corpse a meticulous examination. "Look what I found in his back. A knife and I'd say it was in at least six inches. Yours, Mr. Bond?"

"Hell no."

"Wait, there's a name on the hilt. 'Property of Colonel Stuart Bentall, M.I. 5.' I remember him; British agent. But he's been dead for ten years. Which means this baby's been toting a pigsticker in his back since 1956 or earlier. I guess one of our bullets must have driven the point into a vital organ."

Bond was kneeling by the two dead men near the Togliatti. "Not a mark on the Dagro. He must have succumbed from fright. Dagroes can't take it too well. Other one looks like a Bulgar or maybe a Bulgro. I got him all right. My initials, I.B., are in his forehead."

"Hey, Mr. Bond! You've been hit."

Goshen's giant saw Bond touch the sticky mess dribbling from his side and a profound sadness humanize the cruelly handsome face. "It's my waistcoat, made of bleeding madras," Bond said. "It took the brunt of the knife, saved my life." He cradled the garment in his muscular arms. "Any plasma in that chopper?"

"Sorry. No."

Bond walked over to the shame-faced CIA man. "Not your fault, buddy boy. You couldn't have known. Anyway it's too late." He knelt, scooped a hole in the sand and placed the waistcoat inside. "You know any decent words to say in Hindi or Urdu? No? Well, I'll just say something from my heart, that's all." He looked at the forlorn little mound of sand. "You were a good waistcoat. If there's some kind of a Laundromat for waistcoats where gentle non-Communist Chinks never use harsh detergents, I hope that's where you're headed. Shalom."

He picked up his Hickok belt and Korvette's luau car coat. "Since I owe you my life I guess introductions are in order, partner. But you know me already." His grin was boyish, guilty. "Goshen didn't trust me, huh?"

The rugged CIA agent shrugged. "Well, you know Goshen." He profferred a shovel-sized hand. "Name's James Brown, CIA Agent Seven-Eleven. The bigot who assigned me that number said it was a *'natural'* because so many of my people are expert crapshooters."

"Makes no difference to me, Jimbo," Bond said. "I read *Ebony* Magazine all the time; Willie Mays is my favorite ballplayer, and if a fine, cleancut Negro moved next door, say a Diahann Carroll, Nancy Wilson, Lena Horne, Barbara McNair, or a Leslie Uggams, I sure as hell wouldn't go running to a realtor with a 'for-sale' sign in my hand."

"You're an okay 'fay." Brown's initial wariness was gone, dissipated by the Israeli's frank, hardhitting clarification of his position.

"And you're okay too—in spades," Bond flipped back, drawing a hearty cackle. "You look like a real specimen, Brown. About six-three, I'd say, 225 pounds. Hell, man, you look like you ought to be full-backing for some pro team at six yards a carry. How did you get into this lousy business?"

Brown lit a Waterford and sighed. "Man, that's real water! Well, seems the CIA had sort of a sociological problem. As you know we're divided into White and Black categories, the former signifying the people in desk jobs, the latter the rough-stuff boys. Someone noticed there wasn't a single black in the Black, so they started shopping around for a token operative. They'd been impressed by the under-cover and often violent aspects of the job I'd been doing in civilian life —registering Negro voters in Mississippi. And the guy who made me Seven-Eleven said, 'Now we got a *real* shadow for the tag jobs.' Let's skip that for now. So you're really going to bust into Shivs?"

"Got to," Bond said, his jaw muscles bulging. He filled James Brown in on the caper, including his showdown with James Bund, threw in the *Loxfinger* and *Matzohball* sagas, but left out the detailed descriptions of the episodes with Liana and Indira and his entire sexual history. No sense cluttering up Brown's head with irrelevant information, he reasoned.

"I can't say as I blame you. But I hope you don't mind if I backstop you again. Orders."

"You might come in handy, Jimbo. I've a homer capsule in mah chit'lin's. Can you track me from outside the walls?"

"Sure. I've got a gadget. If I hear your beep go to sleep I'll assume something's awry."

They got into the MBG. Bond used Button 61 to lob a brace of Calgrenades, ¾-zis force, which blew the Togliatti and the helicopter to bits. "Can't leave a messy desert, Jimbo. Let's go."

"Hold it, Bond. I have some data on the joint that might prove helpful. When your people told Goshen of the TUSH setup here he thought we ought to find out more. So I went pub-crawling in Baghs-Groove last night and the fourth dive paid off. I found a Hungro pretty well in his cups."

"A Hungro?"

"Part African, part Magyar. They tend to be moody, weepy types, big boozers. I got a manual on 'Oppo Mixed Breeds' that has all this crap, incidentally. Well, this one was a room service waiter at Shivs and he just couldn't stand confinement any more so he sneaked out through the rear gate, possibly by bribing a Bulgro . . . they're always on the take, you know . . . and went on a bender. 'Course I helped him along with a few shots of *zuki;* that's the native beer made from stagnant well water and decomposed Buick fan belts. And earlier today I took these from the chopper." He took a manila envelope from his trenchcoat, opened it and spread some aerial photos on the front seat. "The Hungro said the top floor here is for the personal use of the Shivs directorate. There's a conference room here and the rest are individual suites for Auntie and Heinz Sem-Heidt, Holzknicht, and the other seven. Third floor's for the household guard and the service corps. Second's for selected guests, big spenders who get free lodging and eats—no bargain 'cause Shivs gets it all back and then some in the casino, which is on the first floor. Heinz runs the LaGuerre Room. He wins big, too. Seven other krauts run the rest of the gambling. Only Auntie and Holzknicht are never found in the casino. God knows what she does. He's got some kind of a lab upstairs where he fools around. One bit of good news—there are no Swegroes inside Shivs 'cause they might scare the customers away and the help, too. Bulgars, Bulgroes, Dagroes, Spigroes, Spigars . . . they do the strongarm work. And then they have the dogs."

"Dogs?"

"Yup. Hohenzollerns."

"Jesus!" All right, buddy boy, Bond excoriated himself. So they have Hohenzollerns. And maybe more awful beasties that go bump in the night. You didn't think you were going to hear Ronald Reagan do readings from Zane Grey, did you?

"In front of Shivs is the guest area, swimming pool, patio, bar, etc. As you can see it's rather small in comparison to the rest of the grounds. It's closed off by a twenty-foot-high Papuan ironwood fence. I guess the management doesn't want them snooping around the rest of the estate. As for internal security, you just must assume the rooms are bugged and that every non-guest hasn't got your personal interest at heart. I have, though. If I can't hear your belly beeping 'I've Got You Under My Skin' I'm coming in."

CIA Agent Brown's account of the horrors within those walls cast a pall over both of them as they motored silently on, their eyes peering through the mist along the shore for the first glimpse of the witch's lair.

"Stop 'er, Mr. Bond." Fear constricted the voice, robbed it of its robustness. "We're about two hundred yards away. Close enough."

Israel Bond lit a Raleigh and noticed with a sardonic smile that it was the last one in the pack. An omen? The last Raleigh he'd ever smoke? Some people wouldn't consider that prospect the least bit alarming, but they weren't secret agents walking into the mouth of hell. "If I don't make it, Jimbo, you'll find a couple thousand cigarette coupons in the trunk. See that M. gets 'em. And tell her I went out smiling with a Raleigh in my sensual lips. So long, big fella."

He stepped out and saw the brazen windows in the upper floors twinkling a new message: *Come into our parlor, Oy Oy Seven. The spiders are very hungry today.*

Up your glass! The epithet blazed back at them from the grey eyes.

When Bond heard the truck grinding along the sandy path, he crouched behind a clump of spiny *sarajevo* cacti. As it puttered by, he saw the sign on its side, HAJI'S LAUNDRY, and then saw it stop at the rear gate.

Praying the squish, squish, squish of the Andalusian bedsocks on the sand would not be heard over the idling motor, he raced to the back of the truck, his Vicks 44 in his right hand, put the point of it against the lock and blew it off, the Silentium Silencer muffling the discharge. He dove into a pile of something white and fragrant and closed the door behind him, his trained Double Oy nose telling him he had landed on a Rinso wash. Good-o! I've made a clean start!

Bond heard the driver and the guard, the latter's soft, slurring speech indicating its owner was a Bulgro, exchange a few jokes, one of them with the punch line "faggot maggot," and he tore up a Jackie Kannon towel in anger. Goddamnit! That one was getting around too fast! There was no time to pencil the joke out of his notebook of goodies, for the truck was moving again. He heard the ominous clang of the closing gate.

OK, Shivs. I'm inside, he thought. I ask no quarter and I give no quarter.

Then he snickered at his Gung Ho–Don Winslow–Captain Midnight bravado. Big deal! These days, what the hell can you do with a quarter?

20. This Pond's Minus Honey And Almonds

Through a small window in the rear door he could see they were passing through an area darkened by trees and thick foliage. He flung the door open and sprang onto a cobbled roadway, the impact sending a jolt of pain through his Andalusian bedsocks. He heard the clatter of the truck die. All was still, save for the humming of bees, the chirping of "katydid! katydid!" from one part of the forest, a scornful answering, *"Yenteh! Yenteh!"* from another.

The squeak of wheels coming up the path sent him on a headlong dive into the nearest bush. He cursed himself for his precipitance, for he'd landed in a *chipango* plant whose spearlike shoots cut open his right cheek. The smell of his type-A blood sickened and frightened him. What if the dogs scented it?

A spasm went through his body when he heard the doggerel crooned by the iron voice.

> *"Fee, fie, foe, foo,*
> *I smell the blood of a lurking Jew."*

He was looking into the mustard-yellow orbs of Auntie Sem-Heidt.

She sat in her wheelchair, her chalky face looking as though it had been fashioned from a thousand grave-worm bellies sewn together. Her clawlike fingers stroked the life-giving battery on her lap with a repulsive fondness. The wig she had chosen this afternoon was algae green, matched by a similar tint on her lips and a green-and-black housedress. "There is someone in the forest, Heinz."

"Nein, lieber Gerda. A small animal, perhaps, or the wind." Her mate stood by her side, stuffing Burgerbits into his cave of a mouth, his profane blimp of a body garbed in a Bavarian mountain climber's costume, white-lace dickey, red-velvet shorts and suspenders, the piano legs in lederhosen and red-leather Mary Jane sandals. "Let us continue our constitutional."

"Nein, we shall stop here for a moment. Locksley, a muffin, *bitte*."

The dwarf in the jester's outfit seemed pleased at being able to

service his wardress. He took a muffin from her pocket and inserted it
between the electromagnetic coils. Its scent filtered through the shoots
to Bond's nose, enticing at first, then acrid, and he heard Auntie Sem-
Heidt's invectives. "Cursed gnome! You have burned my muffin! Heinz,
my knout!"

The scrawny arm lashed out with surprising power, the metal tip of
the knout thudding against Locksley's back.

"Enough, Gerda. You will kill the creature," Heinz said. "A good
dwarf nowadays is hard to find."

She acknowledged his wisdom. Locksley expressed his gratitude for
the cessation of the flagellation with a cartwheel, during which he
clapped his hands several times. It drew a whinny of approval from
his mistress.

"Your gyrations have pleased me, dear little freak." The claws patted
the puckered apple of a face. "I shall reward you with a chance to see
Auntie Gerda's little toy. Behold!" She spread open the housedress and
the dwarf did a triple cartwheel this time.

Gottenu! The Israeli's grey eyes did cartwheels of their own. Z.'s
voice echoed: "He gave her an external plastic heart and it works."

If his own heart had not been pounding so stridently he would have
heard the rush of air and the snarling "baa-a-a" just before the thing
hit him like a bullet. *Gevaldt!* He could not stifle the cry as the teeth
and horn penetrated his right shoulder. "I was correct!" the iron voice
called. "There is an intruder! The dog has flushed him."

A 135-pound steel-ribbed Hohenzollern, the part-German shepherd,
part-German sheep bred by the S.S. during the 40's in the Mordegruppe
Research Center in the Black Forest for sentry duty and ferreting out
downed Allied fliers, was worrying at his throat, the foul-smelling saliva
now mixed with Bond's blood dripping from the fangs. He could see
the orange and black coat and the thick white mushroom of wool on
its skull, the hard lance of a unihorn—Hohenzollerns, nervous, un-
stable, as apt to tug out a friend's throat as an enemy's.

Man and beast were rolling over and over, both raked by spines and
shoots, the former's right elbow taking the fury of the teeth. Bond's left
hand grasped the stem of the woolen mushroom and pulled it over the
creature's mad-dog eyes, blinding it for a vital second, then with a
superhuman effort drove the animal against the trunk of a tree. There
was a yelp and the spine snapped.

Ignoring the claret pouring out of his mangled arm and shoulder, he
ran deeper into the brush, for a chorus of baa-a-as told him the whole
pack had been set loose on his bloody trail. There was a thrashing
sound, a slurring Bulgro voice: "He went this way!" An angry Dagro's,
"No, you stupid bastard, the other way."

Gottenu! Fire ants, crazed by the odor of blood, were sliding down
little poles and swarming out of their hills. He brushed a loathsome
phalanx off his body, not before the industrious pincers had carved
out another chunk of shoulder.

THIS POND'S MINUS HONEY AND ALMONDS

"Bear left!" It was the gravelly command of a Bulgar. Bond ducked behind a tree and saw a hawklike face emerge over the foliage and stiffen into a sneer when a Spigar voice somewhere piped out: "No, he doubled back, you —— clod!"

It was quite apparent these hired thugs despised each other. By thunder, he'd use that ill feeling against them!

He sent out a slurring shout. "Hey, man, where you come off callin' me a stupid bastard? I don't take that —— from nobody, 'specially a lice-ridden Dagro!" He pitched his voice higher. "Ain't no stinkin', garlic-chompin' Spigar gonna tell us Dagroes what to do. We got the brains in this outfit, man; you ain't nothin' but low-class dung; you ain't fit to sleep with a Swegro; you lower than a Bulgar's bunions; you smell like a Hungro sittin' in nine-week-old goulash." He simulated a gravel-throated tirade next: "What —— dares compare a pure Bulgar with the rest of you half-breed carrion? Death to Spigars, Hungroes, Spigroes, Dagroes! Mere total paralysis to Bulgroes, who at least had enough sense to be born part Bulgar!"

Full-scale insurrection broke out in ten seconds. He could hear vile imprecations and knew his stratagem had worked. The hunters had become the hunted! Dagro knives slashed Bulgar bodies; Spigroes clubbed Bulgro heads; Spigars and Hungroes traded blasts with sawed-off mortar pistols. Everywhere was the smell of cordite, Woolite, claret and death.

But he heard the baying of the Hohenzollerns and he trembled as he pushed his torn body through cacti, thornbushes, and Wilkinson sword-grass, his Korvette's luau car coat in shreds. The terrain grew soft, then—splash!—he was knee-deep in a slimy pond, its muddy brown slowly stained red by his dripping wounds. Brown, red . . . and now— silver! A silvery mass darting across the water—Gottenu!—voracious yellow teeth were ripping into his legs. He fell to his knees, took another bite on his hand which severed his beloved 30-year-old Irving Caesar Sing a Song of Safety Club ring. It fell into the murky waters, lost forever.

Somehow he managed to stumble to the other side, avoiding the snapping jaws of a jacare, the Brazilian crocodile, which he dispatched by emptying all of his Vicks 44 slugs into its eyes. There was no time to skin the creature to compensate himself for part of this ordeal by treating himself to a fine pair of Amazonian bedsocks (150 quasars retail if they were a farthingale) because the red-eyed, steel-fanged Hohenzollerns, six of them, came through the thicket to the opposite side of the pond. "What a croc!" he said, looking at the body of the slain jacare with regret, and turned to meet the new challenge.

Though they growled and thrust at the air with their unihorns, they did not charge across the pond. They know what's in there, he thought. Got to make 'em mad enough to come over. Another psychological warfare bit?

"You yellow, lily-livered Deutsche hunds . . . come and take a Jew

—if you can! Come on, krauts. I've seen chihuahuas that could kick the crap out of the whole bunch of you." One braced to spring; an older, wiser head bit into its tail to restrain it.

Bond spoke a flat, pedantic sentence. "According to the better trade magazines, the Renault outperforms the Volkswagen in every way."

Now there was no holding them back. The impetuous one left his tail in the older Hohenzollern's mouth to lead the charge, blood gushing from his hind quarters. They followed suit, eyes rolling with insensate hatred, coming on for the kill. They never reached him. One by one they were savaged by the silvery mass, howling in agony as they went under; again the water swirled with red and pink.

Pieroghana! the flesh-loving Polish devilfish of the Vistula River, known to drag down careless fishermen, pleasure boats and, in three recorded instances, governments. . . .

"Dobzheh, dobzheh!"* He collapsed.

21. For "The Clipper" And "Mighty Mick"

It was the iron voice somewhere close by—"Heinz! Release the birds!" —that told him he dare not linger another second. He staggered blindly into the forest again until—thump!—his head rammed into something hard, the Papuan ironwood fence James Brown had indicated to him on the map. Beyond it he could hear brittle laughter and splashing. He knew the relative safety of the guest area could be his, if he could scale it.

How?

Fool that he was, he was leaning on the answer—a bamboo tree. He jerked one of its stems back and forth until it cracked explosively. Balancing it between his hands he backed off about thirty feet. There came the whirring of wings; he turned to see a formation of diving condors, then the mesmeric yellow eyes of Auntie Sem-Heidt as the wheelchair pushed by the straining Locksley came into view. Her hand flicked out, the knout's steel tip catching Bond between the shoulder-

* Good, good!

blades, but he was rushing toward the twenty-foot-high barrier, thrusting the bamboo pole into the earth, arching his body over its top as talons and bullets reached for him in vain. He was soaring up, up, up over the ironwood stakes, whose discolored points meant certain death by curare, fugu or Noxon if they scratched the tiniest hole in his epidermis. He was vaguely conscious of the fact that he had broken the world's pole-vaulting mark by a foot or more (with an old-fashioned bamboo pole, not one of those hopped-up Fiberglass jobs) but he put the feat out of his mind, for now, the black-green netherworld behind him, Israel Bond was descending into the opulent section reserved for the big spenders; well-manicured lawns, flowerbeds and a circular pool around which sat potbellied men in the company of tanned, supple goddesses in bikinis being served drinks by dark little men flashing obsequious, gold-toothed smiles.

His feet thudded into a pudgy back, sending one of the male guests sprawling into the pool, the klonk of skull against diving board fortuitously smothered by the splashes of frolicking guests, and Bond flopped into a Norman Hekler-designed Jivaro lounging chair next to a splendidly proportioned auburn-haired enchantress who did not look up as she commented in an offhand manner, "That was my husband, Count Amontillado Di Terrazzo-Crotchetti, you just knocked into the pool. He cawn't swim, y'know."

"Pity," Bond said. Then—"Tracy! Tracy!"

The face was bored no more. "Iz! Iz, my darling!" The wonderfully wanton jet-setter who had shared that memorable summer with Bond at Portofino buried her fine, white teeth into his shoulder, the torn one. "Oh, my darling. You're hurt. And what are you doing here?"

One of the poolside waiters came to the table. "Pardonnez-moi, Countess. This gentleman—" the lips smiled; the eyes were hostile—"is a friend of yours? You are cognizant of the by-laws of Shivs regarding non-members and interlopers."

"A very dear, dear friend, Valdespino. This is Mr.— " She felt his urgent hand upon her thigh, saw a signal in the grey eyes—"Mr. Dalby, Larrimore Dalby, of Dalby & Ross, my suture future brokers. Good man to know if you're trying to corner the suture market, Valdespino."

The eyes remained suspicious. "I have a sorrowful announcement, madam. The count has drowned."

"A tragic loss, Valdespino. Let's have a round of drinks to his memory. I'll let Mr. Dalby order." She shot Bond a challenging glance.

Still wants to know if I've got the old expertise, he mused. He looked at his watch. "Well, Valdespino, it's 4:30, too early for the Dom De-Luise '17 which must never be served in the heat of the day, too late for the Armand Ruderman '25, which is at its effervescent best only between 9 and 11 A.M., and then only if served within four hundred miles of either side of the International Date Line (her eyes were filled with veneration, the mouth moistening with lust) so let's just make it two Good Old 'Arolds, with either the Lavagetto '38 or the Cavaretta '40, spiced by Wink, the saucy one from Canada Dry. Meet with your approval, Valdespino?"

"Oui, monsieur. The *drinks* meet with my approval." He went to fetch them, his cold eyes still on Bond.

He practically italicized the word "drinks," Bond thought. (He could not know the italicization was literal.) They meet with his approval, but I don't. He kept looking at the blood on my shoulder. I'm going to have trouble with this little man.

"Bless you for the little white lie, dearest Tracy." He painted the oval cheeks red with an affectionate squeeze of his bloody hand.

"Oh, it'll cost you, Iz, don't worry." She ran her cool hand over the corrugated muscles of his navel. "What are you doing here anyway, Mr. . . . uh . . . Dalby?"

"Freelance writing job. Sneaked in to get some data on a piece to be called 'Gambling, Armageddon of the Soul,' which I hope to peddle to *The Watchtower* Magazine."

"You're lying, Iz—uh, Larrimore. I've suspected for some time you're one of those secret agents . . . those nights in Portofino when the shoulder holster pressed against my body as we made love . . . the times you'd jump up from some nightmare yelling 'SMERSH! SWISH! TUSH!' and start firing that damn gun all over the place. I never told you about the killings of bellhops and cleaning women I had to hush up with my husband's money."

"Okay, so you know. Keep it down, bright eyes. There are mikes hidden all over the place."

"If you're here to probe the evils of gambling, my pet, why don't you take a gamble and discuss them with me at full length . . . on my full-length bed? Room 25, second floor."

"Logical way to get into the subject," Bond jested. "Let's away, shall we?" First he took out his Inca-Dinca silver cigarette case and fumbled with a Raleigh so he could keep it open a few seconds longer. The interior mirror caught Valdespino behind a palm tree, popping a capsule between the white and gold teeth. Planting a homer capsule in himself like mine, Bond realized. Señor Valdespino is going to tag me all over the joint. Bet somebody in Shivs at a master controlboard right now is getting a beep-beep-beep on the personal frequency assigned to Valdespino, which tells him Valdespino suspects something. "Second thought, Tracy, I'll meet you at the room a little later. Keep the home fires burning."

"They are now," she panted. "Don't you dare forget me, you mother-stoker."

Bond walked toward the villa, smiling at the oafish klomp-klomp-klomp of footsteps behind. A clumsy tag job . . . you never tag a man in Father & Son croco-mocs, Señor Slewfoot.

He nodded to the blah guests on the porch, went inside and found the Herr O' the Hund Cocktail Lounge to the right of the main desk. "Seven and Seven," he told the sleepy-eyed Bulgro behind the bar polishing the Dixie Cups.

"Fourteen." Then the man, suddenly aware of the fact he was not being given a math quiz, blushed in the adorable way that all rattled Bulgroes do. "Sorry, sir. I'll make one up right away."

"Better make that two Seven and Sevens. I've got a friend coming in. Hi, Valdespino," he said with an airy wave. "Join me for a little drinkie-poo?"

The sheepish waiter decided to brazen it out. "If you wish, sir, though it is against Shivs' policy for the help to fraternize. . . ."

"No buts about it, old man. I insist. About time hard-working little waiters got waited on themselves, huh?" Bond picked up the two drinks, letting the anti-homer capsule capsule fall from his palm into Valdespino's. "Down the hatch, fella." He experienced a thrill as the man drained his drink. He started to down his own when the Bulgro said, "That'll be three quasars and six, sir." Bond dug out a five-quasar note and walked over to the bartender. "Keep the change. And here's an extra colodny just for the way you blush."

The mistake was turning his back to Valdespino, long enough for the little man to place a pellet into Bond's half-finished libation. Bond came back to belt it down, said flippantly, "Nice talking to you lads," and went back into the lobby. He ambled down a corridor into the casino past a number of guests in Bermuda Schwartz shorts, hot-eyed degenerate gamblers who stuffed farthingales into a battery of machines. One screamed, "I hit! I hit!" and Bond saw the man's shaky hands receive a pack of Luckies.

He did not know what made him turn his head; intuition, perhaps; whatever it was, it saved his life. The knife whistled by, burying itself into the heart of a rose on the damask-covered wall. His hands flew to his mezzuzah, the cylindrical symbol of his faith on a chain around his neck, and, with a long, tapering finger on the Star of David, he aimed it at Valdespino who was pulling another knife from his cummerbund. But the second knife fell from the man's hand, the Molochamovis-B tipped needle from the mezzuzah flew far from its intended mark, killing the unfortunate chap who'd beat Shivs' one-armed bandit for the cigarettes. Bond and Valdespino were doubled up, their hands clutching their stomachs, water streaming from their eyes. They began a frantic race toward a door with a painting of a haughty cavalier on it, cursing and shoving each other aside. Then they were in the room, felling two elderly gentlemen about to go into the stalls with hammer blows, and, at last, in the stalls, Hickok belt and cummerbund falling to the floor. From the groans of Valdespino and his own Bond knew they had both been victimized by anti-homer capsules of similar potency.

"Truce," he gasped and heard a weak, "Oui, monsieur."

He lit a Raleigh. "Smoke, Valdespino?" He heard a grunt he took to be yes and shoved one underneath the partition with a blue-tipped Ohio match.

"Merci."

"That's quite a device you put into me, old man. A Dr. Holzknicht special?"

"Indeed, sir." Valdespino sighed. "And—oooh—may I compliment you on the efficacy of the one you placed in my drink, sir."

"Fella named Lavi HaLavi's responsible for—" He could not finish the sentence.

Some time later, the fight drained out of them, they were engaged in an amiable chat, Bond admiring the Polaroid photos of Valdespino's wife and three children his former adversary had passed to him. "Nice young 'uns, Valdespino. Though I'd hate to entrust their future to the kind of megalomaniacs you've thrown in with."

With one of his trenchant analyses of the political forces shaping the world's destiny, coupled with an offer of a CIA job for 25 percent more than TUSH was paying (plus hospitalization, old-age benefits and a tour of Disneyland; he was sure Goshen would make good on all counts) he persuaded Valdespino to change sides. As they washed up, he told the waiter, "You won't be sorry, old chap. The CIA can always find a spot for an ugly, clever little knife-throwing fanatic."

"Mon Dieu!" Valdespino was suddenly pale. "I have been guilty of the worst sort of amateurism." He made a hasty search through the cubicles. "Look, Mr. Bond, in each roll of ultra-soft, irritant-free Delsey. Listening devices. In Shivs, sir, even the stalls have ears. They have heard my betrayal. It is all over for me. Get out while you can."

Gottenu! Bond slapped his forehead. "I've also forgotten. My buddy, CIA Agent James Brown, is out there. Now that he isn't getting the signal he'll be barging in."

They headed through the casino to the lobby. Through the loudspeaker they heard shouts in a sort of doubletalk Bond assumed was a code for Shivs' personnel.

"Mr. Bond, they are ordering their men to get the guests back into the casino on some pretext or other—free hot milk and cookies, I think. Which means they don't want witnesses around when they open the front gate to admit your friend, whom they have spotted. He, too, is a goner. They will cut him down. I have just heard my name mentioned as well, sir, in a most unfavorable light."

"Got to warn him, Valdespino. Is there any—"

Valdespino would be of benefit no more. He fell on his face, a machete vibrating in his back. Down the corridor flew a trio of Shivs' house police, two Bulgars and one that looked like a cross between.... What does it matter *what* breed he is, you idiot! Bond swore at himself. Run! Run!

He lurched back into the lobby, firing the mezzuzah's auxiliary needle into the desk clerk's cheek, the nerve poison doing its job in 1.9 seconds. He crouched behind the front desk, discovered some bars of

Camay on a bottom shelf and jammed them into the pockets of his Korvette's luau car coat. No reason why a secret agent has to have rough, red hands, unless, of course, he's an Apache, Bond reasoned. When he pushed the bars into the right-hand pocket a long, tapering finger hit the round, hard thing.

Little Rickey Bond's Superball! Damn it, he'd forgotten to give it back to Milton's kid after that swell game of catch in Trenton . . . sixty billion miles and years away. Without knowing why, he let his mind wander back to that catch. He'd seen how Superball, the latest toy sensation, could outbounce by a 50 to 1 ratio the ordinary balls he'd used as a youngster.

He knew now how to warn CIA Agent James Brown, but it might prove fatal. The hell with the risk! With his "Old Wrangler" Ralston Straight-Shooter knife he cut a message into the ball: TRAP! STAY OUT! BRING HELP! BUY AN ISRAEL BOND! In his mind's eye he saw the front porch of Shivs facing the front gate, perhaps 600 feet away, and himself as a fourteen-year-old would-be Joltin' Joe D. back in Trenton, hurling his moth-eaten tennis ball against the porch of his Union Street home in the game known variously as "pinnerball," "stoopball," or "porchball."

He knew they'd be waiting for Brown; so they were, their gimlet eyes at the sights of Manicottis trained on the gate. There would be time for one drive only against the "pinner" or point of a porch step. Now! He charged down the steps and stooped into position. "Der Jude! Take him!" The iron voice . . , he tore his grey eyes away from the horrid yellow ones and swung his usable left arm on a downward slant, felt a grand old-time tingle as the ball kissed the point and took off like an angelic thing, up, up, up, a black dot tickling the underbelly of a cloud, then over the hundred-foot wall with plenty to spare, the tape measure blast of all tape measure Ballantine blasts, a Yankee Stadium roof-clearing thing of beauty, and he could see in the center of the explosions in his head the faces of DiMag and Mantle smiling a "well done, fella" and hear his own stammered reply: "That one was for you, Clipper, and you, too, Mighty Mick," before the half-dozen rifle stocks clubbed him into limbo.

22. Good Old Sol*

To his amazement the voice was not iron, the eyes were not yellow, but brown, intelligent, almost sympathetic.

"Let us talk quickly, Oy Oy Seven. There is little time. Even now Gerda is dressing for the extraordinary occasion of inflicting—ah, let us say testing, some unusual devices upon the catch of her lifetime, Secret Agent Israel Bond. Undoubtedly she is putting on her finest housedress and practicing upon Locksley. her dwarf, with a whip she has sworn will be used only upon you, a cat o' twenty-seven tails presented to her by Der Führer (The speaker's hand shot up in a heil) himself. Cooperate with me, Bond, and I will save you from unimaginable suffering. I want to know how much M 33 and ⅓ knows about 'Operation Alienation,' how deeply the CIA is involved, what plans both have for counterattacking, how the new king can best be gotten to and eliminated, as well as a few items to sate my personal curiosity."

Bond, his hands chained to the wall, saw a bland face and the high forehead of the scholar. His questioner was a man of medium height with a military crewcut who wore a white labcoat. Of course—Dr. Ernst Holzknicht, whose mild appearance belied his status as the evil genius behind all of Eretz Israel's woes.

"Where am I, Holzknicht?" He would not give the kraut the courtesy of "Herr Doktor," no matter what the cost. "And remember, under the terms of the Geneva Convention I can only give you my name, rank and Diners Club number."

Dr. Holzknicht blew a mouthful of Muriel smoke into his face. "You are in the cellar of Shivs, the very room where Oy Oy Five met his end at Gerda's claws, so you see there is no regard for Geneva's niceties here."

Bond inhaled the foul air. "And if I cooperate, then what? Autographed pictures of David McCallum and Robert Vaughn?"

"I will reward you with a quick, painless death, an injection of *diathorenzymesheckeygreen,* and say that you died of your many wounds, which, if you'll notice, I have treated. I have no personal interest in torturing you. It would serve no scientific purpose."

* The chapter title just happened to work out this way. But I can not quarrel with the sentiment.—S.W.

"You're not like the others, Holzknicht. You're a genius of medicine and psychiatry, you don't enjoy sadism, and I see you're wearing a pair of fifty-colodny Dr. Joyce Brothers bedsocks, which means you have a fully developed artistic sensitivity; yet you align yourself with these ghouls. Why?"

"That is a long story, Bond. Ja, I agree; the Sem-Heidts are quite mad. Heinz is a fat-swollen sybarite who lives only for calories and the cheap thrills of the *la guerre* table. Gerda is a monster who must cause some kind of misery every day of her life or she finds life meaningless. I regret that a man of my intellect and taste has been forced to seek alliance with them, but TUSH has power and the finances to underwrite my researches."

"Can't those researches be conducted for some democratic country? I'm sure your past indiscretions would be forgiven."

"You do not fully understand, Bond. The main reason I am with TUSH is because I concur with its ultimate goal. Even as a young scientist I was far ahead of my older, allegedly wiser colleagues in understanding the monumental problems facing mankind. Long ago I foresaw the great upheavals arising from awakened nationalism in the former colonial territories, the impact of the population explosion, the terrible food shortages, automation, water pollution, the threat of attack by aliens from other planets and the ever-growing possibility that the sun may die in five billion years, leaving earth a cold, shriveled, dead mass of rock. With my logical, dispassionate scientist's mind, I arrived at one incontestable solution to all these problems."

"And that is?"

"We have got to destroy all the Jews."

"Well," Bond said uncertainly, "if you put it *that* way"—then he was furious at himself for a momentary weakness—"no, damn it, no! I won't play ball, kraut. Do your worst."

"So? A pity." The doctor sighed. "In that case I shall leave you in the capable claws of Auntie Sem-Heidt. First, however, we shall soften you up." He walked to a corner of the cell and slid open the lid of a screened cage. "Good day, Bond, and goodbye." He was gone.

From the cage came a soft scratching sound . . . then, one by one, out came an abhorrent line of crawling brown things, each about six inches long, with countless little feet and curved claws at each end. Israel Bond felt the hair on the back of his neck—rising!

He was about to be attacked by a miggle of millepedes from the Lesser Antilles.

They moved inexorably toward him. He could pick out the pinpoints of red that were their eyes. Their bites might not mean death, at least the instantaneous kind, just simple agony that would turn his fine black hair white and the dark, cruelly handsome face into a Dorian Gray After within seconds.

In his terror he twisted at his manacles, rubbing huge patches of skin from his wrists; they held. Something clanged against the floor and he realized that in his straining desperation he had snapped the Tuck Tape that bound the Instant Processed Cold Rolled Extra Strength Steel tool to his calf. Alas, it was six inches (the exact length of the filthy stalkers) from his feet. Might as well be six miles, he lamented, as the line of millepedes moved on, now less than a foot away, their claws held high to lance into flesh. He closed his eyes. "Hear O Israel, the Lord Our God, The Lord is One." He waited for the first prickle of millepede feet on his legs, the first claw squirting venom.

What was taking them so long?

He opened his eyes.

They had stopped in their tracks, deploying in battle formation toward the steel-barred opening that served as the cell's only window.

Crawling through the bars, caught by a shaft of fading sunlight, was the enormous, hairy, tarantulalike ant of the Arabian Desert, a sol-pugid, searching for food.

"Solpugid. Sol. Sollie, baby." Thrice he entreated the new arrival in a voice cracking with emotion. "Help me, Sol. Help one of your own who's up against it now. Don't stop to polemicize about Orthodox, Conservative and Reform differences. *Ich bin a Yid,* Sollie. *Du bist aichit. Helf meer!"*

The arachnid seemed to comprehend. It quickened its pace, furry legs impelling it into the midst of the enemy, the terrible jaws scoring direct hits time and again. Three of them were cut in twain, the severed halves thrashing in death throes. But Solpugid had been slashed damagingly by two of them hitting it from both sides in a prearranged pincer plan; its vital juices ebbed from the bites. It drove back at the two attackers, pulling them within the area of the jaws. Bond heard the crunch of the jaws into their carapaces. One left!

"Sol! Behind you!" It spun to meet the sneak attack—too late—and the claw laden with excruciating poison struck home. Solpugid shook the millepede off its back with a mighty heave, which sent it banging into a wall, then chomped it into jagged bits.

Gottenu! Bond thought. It's saved me. Then he felt a new thrill of horror as he heard the elevator whine, bearing, he knew, the Bitch of Schweinbaden.

That damned tool! So near, yet so far.

He looked at the barely alive Solpugid.

"Sol, that hunk of metal. If you've got anything left—push it over to me."

A few of the eyes blinked dully. It's so damn shot through with poison it can't hear me anymore, Bond thought.

Solpugid got up.

With its last atom of power, it staggered up on three of its eight legs (the rest, no doubt, were numbed by the circulating venom), geared itself for a final rush and smashed into the chunk of metal, which, Bond deduced, must have outweighed it 150 times. The tool skipped over the stone, coming to rest against his ankle just as the elevator hit bottom. Bond was in action, kicking off an Andalusian bedsock, pinching the device between his toes, kicking up and catching it with his even, white teeth. He ignored the claret oozing from the corner of his cut sensual mouth, bit harder into the tool and with a series of nods worked it against his bonds. He smelled the burning metal shavings as the IPCRESS file ate its effortless way through the links, and suddenly he was falling on his face as they gave way. No time to crow (he was a poor birdcall imitator anyway)—the squeak of the wheelchair down a cellar corridor and the harridan's cackle were broadcasting a message: Run! Run! Live to fight another day when the odds are better.

"Olav Ha Sholom,"* he whispered to the dead Solpugid, then scraped the IPCRESS file against the bars which crumbled before its ridges. He was halfway through the window when the cell door swung open. "Stop him, Locksley! Stop him!" Her new whip laced Bond's back but he was beyond feeling. With a vicious backward kick he hurled the dwarf, who was attempting to bite his leg, into the wall. Outside, he looked down and balled up his right fist and shook it at the yellow eyes, which gave way for the first time to his grey ones. "You gutter bitch! You'll have a real heartburn before Eretz Israel is through with you!" He fled into the sultry night.

23. First Things Second

On the sound theory that TUSH would expect him to hightail it as far from Shivs as his battered frame could take him, Bond walked coolly up the porch, through the lobby now bustling with guests about to start their night's run at the tables, and, shunning the elevator, went up via the service stairs. His object: the fourth floor and the documents that would incriminate the heinous junta before the whole world.

As he reached the second floor landing he saw a shadow and cocked his left fist for a killing blow. There was a sob and warm arms fell upon him. "Tracy!"

She was naked, atremble; demented eyes rolled in the oval face. "I've been waiting, waiting, waiting! Oh, Iz, Iz, Iz! Hurry, hurry, hurry!"

Well, they say all good things come in threes, he thought, and let her drag him down the hallway into Room 25. It was apparent she had

* Rest in peace.

been champing at (and for) the bit quite awhile. A pile of Viceroy stubs spilled out of an ashtray onto the Du Pont 105 throw rug, the blankets on the Norman Hekler-designed Mr. Greenjeans hide-a-bed were tossed to one side, the phonograph was playing DePussey's "Afternoon of a Nymph."

It was matchless ecstasy for Tracy, so much so that on her roller coaster ride to fulfillment she bit through and tore off from her arm her black mourning band; not for Bond, whose wounds prevented him from reaching that exalted realm, though he did settle for a fuzzy area between sublime rapture and divine consummation.

"Iz." She was sleepy-happy, her oval face glistening with the contentment of a baby who has just guzzled Gerber's Strained Scotch. "Don't leave me ever."

"I must—for now, darling. I've got a big job ahead of me. Sleep and dream of that summer in Portofino. Incidentally, sweet, I've films of that interlude. Would you mind terribly if I had them exhibited at some of the better men's clubs? Gladly share the net receipts with you after the distributor's take."

"Do anything you. . . ." She was asleep.

Sweet kid, Tracy. A *shikseh,* but that could be altered. Man could do worse than end up with her, especially since she was now the sole heir to the count's squeegee empire. Stop the dawdling, Oy Oy Seven, and get up to the fourth floor!

It was deserted, the directors and Heinz Sem-Heidt downstairs running the games. At the conference room door sat a dozing Spigar in a gold lamé frock coat, opera hat and Levi Strauss Harlow bellbottom jeans, a Wickersham-Freehan antelope gun on his lap. From the smell it was obvious the man had been at the *zuki* keg and it was an easy matter for Bond to take the weapon from his hands and bash his head in.

The room held nothing of interest for him except for a few Muriel cigars in a bowl, which he took. He ransacked eight of the directors' suites, again finding nothing rewarding, eschewed a ninth, obviously the doctor's, when he heard the bubbling of some chemical or other. But he received a jolt when he eased open the door to the tenth suite.

She was in the wheelchair, the yellow eyes masked by chalk-white lids on whose surface were branching green and red veins; snores gurgled from the thin nose and blue lips. Her hands rested on the jester's cap of Locksley, who slept in a barbed-wire crib next to the wheelchair, his thumb in his mouth.

Bond tiptoed across the threadbare rug, kicking aside strewn-about housedresses, his grey eyes darting into nook and cranny for the documents. On the walls he saw shelves lined with her personal library—*A Child's Garden of Perversion, Jayne's Fighting Whips of the World 1965–66, Flay Your Way To Contentment, De Sade—He Really Knew How to Hurt a Guy*—and a pennant, SCHWEINBADEN, CAMP OF THE MONTH FOR THREE STRAIGHT YEARS.

And then he found it—behind her ermine-trimmed iron Maiden Lady—the safe. He prayed the tom-tom that was his heart would not rouse the hag as he pulled the sandpaper from his hip pocket and sensitized the tips of his long tapering fingers. Click! The first tumbler —five minutes passed—click!—the second—good-o! He glanced at the radioactive dial on his shockproof Kissling. Nine-twenty. In another ten minutes the safe would yield its treasure. By nine-thirty the proof of the existence of Operation Alienation would be in his hand.

Nine-thirty!

Gottenu!

She would be at the oasis at nine-thirty, his own and only true love, Sarah Lawrence of Arabia!

Well, Oy Oy Seven, what comes first, your personal happiness or the destruction of the powers of darkness?

Certainly, he told himself as he bounded down the stairs and through the lobby, the papers would be there tomorrow, none the worse for a good night's sleep, possibly the better for it, because an old, sleepy-eyed, grouchpuss set of documents wouldn't be disposed to divulge anything significant.

He chopped down on the doorman's neck with his stiffened left hand and commandeered a Lincoln Continental convertible, flattening the front gate, two Bulgroes and a Dagro on his juggernaut jaunt to the desert.

A million jewels hung suspended on the black velvet night. Somewhere the Norman Hekler Choir sang a Norman Luboff arrangement of "Stairway to the Stars" to the accompaniment of the Les McCann Trio. One thought plagued him. Would his hot Baronevkeh *shtetl* blood so recently cooled by his encounter with Countess Tracy be revived with a flash from the dark eyes of the mystery woman? Or would he prove a dismal failure and break her heart? *Gottenu,* he prayed, my kingdom for six dozen oysters laced with Gallo Wine!

He need not have worried, for as he parked the MBG under the palms he heard the tender *dee dee, da, da, da, da, dee dee* theme (this time a scat version by Joe Carroll; she had cleverly changed tapes for a new dramatic effect) and his body began tingling in all the right places, even in a few new ones he had never dreamed were zones of erogeneity, the tips of his Andalusian bedsocks and the loops of his Hickok belt.

The white camel poked its nose over the dune and the cool musical voice said, "Come, Mr. Bond. My desert is waiting." No second invitation was required. He crashed through the windscreen, paying no heed to the new cuts and bruises, and slid down its bonnet to the lukewarm sand. Now he was on Latakia, enclasping her waist, thrilling to her whispered: "Blue heaven and you and I."

"And sand kissing a moonlit sky," he breathed. "Miss Lawrence, will you convert to my faith, marry me and set me up in business?"

"Yes, yes, oh yes!"

He hurled her off Latakia into the dune. His sensual lips brushed her eyes and found to his delight her lids were spiced with Murine and ginger from Bali. "Take off your veil, Miss Lawrence, and let me see the seventh heaven of seventh heavens."

The voice was pleading. "Nay, let us preserve the illusion of this first night between us, Mr. Bond, I pray you."

"I accede, my sweet. Does that restriction apply to your golden robe as well?"

She trembled. "It is yours to do with as you wish. Lift it."

"Miss Lawrence, not that it matters since I am a man of the world, but will I be the first?"

"Would that I had saved myself for you, dearest. Alas, no. There was one other, a ship that passed in the night just once. In America some years ago I went to a John Cage Music Festival in Pough-keepsie. . . ."

Bond scowled. "The third coal scuttle player?"

"Yes. But how. . . ."

"Button your lip, you f—— loose-moraled wench! Let's make it!" He heard his spiteful words echoing in his fine, intelligent ears and was ashamed. "Forgive me, Sarah Lawrence. It doesn't matter. I love you."

His long, tapering fingers drew warmth from her thighs.

"One question, Israel Bond. I know you love me, but why do you want to climb upon my body?"

It came out of him with passionate conviction.

"Because . . . because it is there."

A modest moon blushed and slipped behind the dune, and, as his thighs conquered hers, she emitted a last heated word.

"Ra-a-aw——*ther!*"

24. Sermon On The Mount

He awoke with the first heat of day to find the note pinned to the belt of his sunslax.

"My dearest, dearest, adored one. How can I ever convey the gratitude of a girl who has been taken beyond the boundaries of all that is man's to know? There is an old proverb. 'Every five hundred years the great *ookaloptishman* bird flies out of a secret passage in the tomb of Nofkeh-titi the Ninth and devours a single grain of the Arabian Desert's sand, then disappears back into the recesses of that sacred burial place. When that bird has eaten the desert's last grain of sand and is taken to the Great Academy of Medicine at Khartoum for a high colonic, then one second of eternity will have elapsed.' I shall love you for *all* of eternity, Israel Bond. Until that glorious day when we are made one under the traditional canopy of your faith . . . and I have already committed to memory the Aleph-Baze and three of the five books of Moses . . . I remain yours completely——Sarah Lawrence of Arabia."

On the way back to the palace an elated Israel Bond sang the joyous, wild songs of his childhood, *I Took My Girl to the Enginehouse, She Was a Lulu, Country Boy, Country Boy, Sittin' on a Rock,* his heart pumping the electrifying news: She's mine! She's mine!

In fact, those were the first words he cried as he saw Neon Zion and Monroe Goshen sitting by the great pool, their heads down, their eyes those of beaten dogs.

"Congratulations." Goshen's comment was dry, insincere.

"Come on, Monroe. You can do better than that for an ol' buddy about to kick the bachelor habit. How about you, 113?"

Neon turned his face away from Bond and kicked a Great Northern Hotel auk to death.

"Iz," Goshen said with resignation. "While you were running off half-cocked and unauthorized after TUSH and your lady fair, the king was kidnapped."

Gottenu! Bond slapped his forehead. "How?"

"Bunch of guys in white burnooses, the Wheys, stormed in with guns and took him to a court of judgment at their camp. 'Pears someone told 'em he's a phony. They're going to try him, then behead him. I don't think even the Lawrence dame can get him out of this one."

Back in the MBG, Bond wallowed in self-loathing as Neon and Goshen continued their "Coventry." I've done it this time, he thought, fouled up the assignment, failed to get the goods on TUSH. Beame was right; I've had it with M 33 and ⅓. Win, lose or draw, this is the last caper, Oy Oy Seven.

Only James Brown, at the wheel, had a friendly word. "Man, that vitamin-enriched ball of yours saved my tail, Mr. Bond. I read the good word and made tracks fast—you know my race is born with that natural sense of fear. But when we came back in force, you were off the grounds. TUSH was very cooperative, very, but they'd never heard of you, of course. All traces of your visit had been cleaned up. And while we were there, the Wheys took LeFagel."

Brown had the MBG at an impossible 289.7 hectares, liquefying the road surface, until he pulled into the encampment of a thousand white tents. They got out, arms held high judiciously, covered by stone-faced sentries with Zaparosti-Curtises. "Take us to the king," Bond demanded. "There is no king," one spat, "just an impostor. Follow me, infidels."

More inflammatory TUSH agitprop, Bond figured. Thanks to Sarah, it didn't work on the Kurds, so now they've poisoned the Wheys.

In the center of a circle of thousands of men in white burnooses sat LeFagel, his hands fluttering. "Save me, Super-Semite, save me!" An aged warrior, obviously the muktar* of the tribe, called out scornfully. "What is the judgement of the Wheyan people?"

"Death! Death! Death!" The verdict rasped out of thousands of throats. *Gottenu!* Bond thought. If I had the Luden's franchise I'd leave this enclave a multimillionaire.

"The pretender will be given the opportunity to make a final statement," said the muktar.

LeFagel drew himself up, a new dignity in his bearing. Good-o! Bond thought. It may be the end but he's going out like a man. My tutelage has not been for naught.

"In my final moments I have composed a poem," said the king.

> " 'Looking death in the face I find something more,
> 'Than the River Styx boatman who refuses to accept my
>   Cunard Line credit card . . .
> 'Or grinning skulls welcoming me to the abyss,
> 'The joint of no return,
> 'Or dancing devil dolls by unholy firelight,
> 'Prating of unspeakable terrors to come,
> 'No, I find something more meaningful than this,
> 'I find the beanbag I lost as a child,
> 'And finding a beanbag is death.' "

Even the muktar seemed impressed as he dragged the ax along the sand, the blade cutting a furrow to LeFagel, who knelt to receive it across the back of his neck.

Now it was lifted high, its frightening symmetry caught by the sun. . . .

Dee dee, da, da, da, da, dee dee. . . .

Crack! The ax flew out of the muktar's hands.

Sarah Lawrence of Arabia, astride Latakia, those black eyes at the sights of a Congoleum-Nairn-516 elephant gun, broke through the circle of white-burnoosed tribesmen to reach LeFagel's side.

"Before ye dare spill the truly royal blood of Hakmir's son, I would beg for a boon," she said. "I have brought a great, wise holy man with me, who has been touring our land with his spiritual cavalcade. True, he is not of your faith, but he speaks for all mankind with a transcendent message of universality. Listen as I translate his words, then decide if you are to murder your rightful ruler." She beckoned and a

---

* Balaboss.

little wrinkled man in a Krass Brothers white linen suit, string tie and eleven-gallon Tex Ritter hat entered on an imposing Arabian steed.

By thunder! Bond thought. It's Oral Vincent Graham,* the tent evangelist, the man who stirred the world's heart just before the climactic showdown with Loxfinger in the Red Sea! But can even *his* words still the enmity in this tension-charged situation?

Oral Vincent Graham stood in the stirrups, his keen eyes gauging the hostile mood of the bloodthirsty crowd. He would have to choose his words well. A king's life hung in the balance.

"Whomsoever gainsayeth the measure of men? Yea, whomsoever gainsayeth? Dare ye of small measure gainsay what is not man's to gainsay?"

He paused to let his statement sink in; a wave of angry muttering assailed his ears. They were stirred up! Good!

"The days of the years are as threescore and ten; to the more fortunate, tenscore and three. Wherefore walketh he who gainsayeth not? To green valleys and lush fields, sayeth the sages, yet do not even the sages gainsay and not sayeth? *Sometimes?*

"Pride goeth before a fall, yea, and so doth summer. In the winter of our years we seek the summer, gainsaying it when we can, not gainsaying it when we cannot. Who among ye strays from righteous gainsaying, who dares to number among his summers threescore and ten of straying, gainsaying, measuring and scoring?"

Bond could hear Sarah Lawrence sobbing. He knew the tears were soaking into the veil; his own cheeks were wet.

"Lest ye who would be judged e'en to the measure of the days of your years, beware! Hist! Even to thy children's children and thy children's children's children. For the sins of the father delight the father. Hist! Lest ye hist in haste! If a man walketh not alone can it not be truly said that he is with someone? Whether in vales or fields?

"Oh, my friends, hist and harken. Let it not be said, I say unto you —LET IT NOT BE SAID!" He closed his eyes. "Amen."

Even as the skies echoed the last crescendo of his wrath (bouncing his words off both vales and fields), the muktar and his people were kneeling before LeFagel, smothering his hands with kisses. "Forgive us, O glorious planter of a thousand irrigated opium fields!" The king placed his hand upon the weeping muktar's head. "You are forgiven, muktar; now go make peace with the Kurds and together we shall go on with the winning of the East."

Bond's first impulse was to rush to Sarah Lawrence of Arabia's side, but he saw her riding off into the sunset, her head bowed in thankful supplication. "See you at the dune, baby!" he shouted.

The ride back to Hakmir's palace was exuberant, LeFagel leading the

---

* Incorrectly identified as Oral Graham Vincent in *Loxfinger.* There were numerous errors involved with *Loxfinger,* the most glaring, some felt, the decision to publish it.

chorus of applause for the little evangelist, who kept insisting he had not done anything to deserve it. "Speech wasn't even mine, Mr. Bond. I must 'fess up. I cribbed it verbatim from an obscure little volume called *Thoughts for Alternate Thursdays* by some chap I never even heard of. Name of Lavi HaLavi."

Goshen put his hand in Bond's. "Guess we all owe you an apology, Oy Oy Seven. Thanks to that quick-thinking filly of yours, King Baldroi is now accepted by all of his people, which scotches at least one half of the TUSH scheme. A united people will see to it their king isn't killed; ergo, TUSH fails, its stock goes down on the Espionage Exchange. Shame you haven't been able to expose the terrible plot against your people, though. Maybe it just isn't in the cards."

Bond shook the little CIA op chief's lapels. "Yes, yes! The cards! The cards!"

"You cracking, Iz?"

"No, Monroe. You said it isn't in the cards, but it *is*—literally. What will happen if I go back in there and take on TUSH at *la guerre,* smash their organization by bankrupting it? How can they pay off their agents and run their vast world-wide network if they're broke?"

Goshen looked into those grey eyes, once again hot with the lust for battle. "You may have something there, Iz. But, my God, man, do you realize the kind of stakes you'd need to play a showdown game with Sem-Heidt? Astronomical."

Bond flashed a hard grin. "Raise it, then, damnit! Your government blows billions trying to ferret out these villains. Let me have that stake, buddy boy, and I'll wreck 'em for all time!"

A slow smile began to steal across the dour, puritanical face. "Sounds crazy, but why not? I'll have to make a call to the Tall Texan, maybe have him cancel the loan to Thailand and send the money your way."

Bond smiled. Good-o! Monroe was on the ball again. By chance he spotted the villa and the smile stiffened, for the sun was flashing another message from the brazen upper windows: *You've been lucky, Oy Oy Seven, but come in here once more and.* . . .

"Stop the car!" Bond cried. He pressed Button 502-A and the 155-mm. came out of the floorboard.

Goshen cringed as he watched Bond, his sensual top lip curled into a sneer, fire round after round at the windows. "You f——- snotty glass, you panes in the ass . . . take that! That! And that!" In seconds the upper windows were blown out and Goshen could see the smoke rising from the roof.

"Got every damn one of them! And I'm coming back to get the rest of you, Shivs! Let the cards fall where they will and may the devil take the hindmost torpedo. . . ."

25. All's Fair, In Love And
"La Guerre"

"I'll need," said Bond, running his fingers over his head, "at least six more coats of Beacon Wax, 113. If you can scrounge up some shellac to mix in with it, fine." Neon left the royal suite to carry out Bond's bidding.

Bond sat in his Arcaro jockey shorts, the bible of the great game, *Scarne on La Guerre,* at his elbow, as he practiced a few exquisite maneuvers, the "Richelieu Riffle," the "Buffalo Shuffle" and the tricky "Crusader's Cut."

Goshen put aside the breezy, informative *National Enquirer,* whose front page featured EDDIE SEZ: IF LIZ WANTED ME BACK I'D GO BACK, BUT NOT UNLESS DICK COULD LEARN TO CARE FOR DEBBIE and MR. ED'S SECRET SHAME. He hurled a packet into Bond's lap. "There's your stake, Iz, eighty billion quasars, which represents the advance the Tall Texan got from his publisher for *The Great Society's Genyewine Coloring Book* and *Games Texas People Play.* As a precaution, I'm coming along with my CIA boys so TUSH won't get any ideas about highjacking the dough—if you win."

Back came Neon with the ingredients. As Bond slipped into his Cy Devore *la guerre* gambling outfit—Sammy Davis blue tuxedo, Levi Strauss' "After Nine" formal Levi's and his last pair of rare, 500-quasar Carpathian bedsocks fashioned from the pelts of werewolf puppies— the industrious 113 worked the mixture into Bond's scalp. "It's hard as a rock, Oy Oy Seven."

Bond sent a stream of Raleigh smoke against the artificial plant in the corner. It shriveled, edges curling, and died. "Let's go."

* * * *

His pudgy hands caressing a pile of fuchsia billion-quasar notes, Heinz Sem-Heidt looked around the table. Ach, the fight was gone from this crowd; they had been no match for his Teutonic precision. In Position One was Baroness Yvette Mimeo, a principal stockholder in the A.B. Dick Company, her sundered skull on the table, claret flowing from a deep fissure. Two and Three were occupied by the Iranian frozen custard magnates, Nassim Zolzein-Shah and his wife, the man obviously dead, the woman a babbling wreck. Four, Five and Six were vacant. The Formosan beef and bean sprout consortium, playing erratically as all Orientals do, had been wiped out early. Two had died from the rigors of the game; the third had decently blown his brains out with the Paul Bines pistol provided by the management. Number Seven, Countess Di Terrazzo-Crotchetti, had lost three billion colodnys and begged off with a headache, promising, however, that an old friend would sit in for her. *Zehr goot!* A new goose to pluck!

Shuffling the six packs of cards that go into each boot, he did not notice the entrance of the lean, dark, cruelly handsome man flanked by a coterie of mean-looking individuals, until the menacing voice shook the 4,800 ounces of flab in his body.

"Position Seven this night will properly be occupied by Oy Oy Seven. Yo challengo banco."

The words hit the crowd like a thunderclap. The bank had been challenged! In ten seconds every gaming room in Shivs was deserted by patrons rushing to witness the drama of a lifetime.

Heinz Sem-Heidt looked into the grey eyes of Israel Bond. The quasar notes fell from his hands.

"Strict rules of Scarne, kraut; triple bidding and the Foch boots. Agreed?"

"Ja." Buckets of sweat rolled down the jellyish jowls. "Herr Zentner," he said to the croupier. "The Foch boots, *bitte*."

Bond lit a Raleigh and watched Zentner place the original combat boots worn by Marshal Foch in the Great War upon the baize cloth and put six packs of cards (examined first by Goshen) into each toe. Two other Germans, Krug and Von Kreel, lugged in the caldron of steaming Cream of Wheat, another vital part of the time-honored ritual.

Zentner placed a bowl of Cream of Wheat in each contestant's left hand, a Foch boot in the right. The crowd ceased its hubbub. *"Monsieurs. C'est——"*

"La guerre!" Bond and his porcine foe screamed it simultaneously, hurling the Cream of Wheat into each other's faces and bludgeoning each other's heads with the Foch boots, which, as they made contact, opened at the toes to permit a pink card to fall onto the baize.

Shaking his head to clear the fuzziness, Bond spoke. "Mine has—let me see—one, two, three, four, five, six black things. Yours has; oh, hell, *you* count 'em, Nazi."

"I see three, possibly four."

"Page eighteen of *Scarne on Counting* states clearly: 'Six beats three, possibly four.' You sure it isn't three *and* four, which would give you an American Totalisator Company aggregate of seven?"

"Nein."

"I said *seven,* not nine, you f——ing kraut! Cheating already?"

When Zentner pointed out Sem-Heidt had meant no, Bond gave a cruel laugh. "OK, fat boy. Shove over two hundred forty billion quasars. Now I'm tripling the triple bid."

"C'est——"

"La guerre!"

Cereal and boots flew unerringly to their targets. Gottenu! Bond thought. Beacon Wax might not yellow my head, but can it take sustained punishment? I feel it starting to crack.

His finger ticked off the red hearts on the left side of the card—four. Were there more? Yes! Two in the center, which gave him a total of six. Now, if only the right side of the card—hallelujah! One, two, three, four more! Without question, he was holding a ten. No, eleven— another red heart had appeared! Uh-uh, buddy boy, there are no elevens. The latecomer is a drop of your type-A blood! "Switchez les boots, Sem-Heidt. Privilege of the challenger. And what's your card?"

"I count four diamonds on my card. Are there more, Herr Zentner? Nein? I have lost again."

As the men exchanged boots, Bond said in a furry voice: "That's two thousand one hundred sixty scullions, uh, billiards——"

"Billions," Goshen corrected him. "Iz, you're way ahead, but you're starting to go round the bend. Quit now before he pounds you into sawdust."

"No, no," Bond argued, his hand to his scalp. "Got to go on till he's busted. His boot was heavier, Monroe. That's why I called a switchez." To Sem-Heidt: "Another triple triple, Nazi."

Cereal flew and boots crashed, Bond trumping Sem-Heidt four more times and soon the Nazi's face was blocked from Bond's view by the latter's mound of 15,553 trillion quasars. "Want to dip into your colodnys now, Heinz?"

"Ja, der colodnys, jüdischer Schweinhund." Despite his staggering deficit, there was supreme confidence on the swollen face. Heinz Sem-Heidt made an undetected move with his right foot, kicking the wastebasket under the table.

With the change of currency, the German's luck changed—and he came up with seven trumps in a row, all on aces of spades, whittling Bond's pile to less than half of his original stake.

Bond's bleary eyes caught the smug satisfaction on the inner-tube lips. Rivulets of claret rolled from his lacerated head onto the baize. Gottenu! Damn near busted—what a rotten run of luck; beaten by seven straight aces of spades.

Hold on! Seven? In a combat boot with six decks of cards that should have six aces of spades? Buddy boy, the Hun is shafting you! And I wouldn't be surprised if Holzknicht gave him some illegal head coating—metal maybe.

Bond squandered 20 billion quasars on the next hand to see how it was being done, incurring a terrible jolt that sent the last fragments of Beacon Wax sliding off his skull onto his claret-spattered Sammy Davis tux. His own boot missed badly, but on his follow-through his blood-shot eye saw the hand snake out of the wastebasket and deposit another ace of spades in Sem-Heidt's hand, good enough to beat his nine of clubs, he knew from past experience.

"I—I feel sick," Bond said and fell over the table, deliberately ramming his torn shoulder into the caldron of hot, bubbling Cream of Wheat.

"Clumsy schwein!" snarled Sem-Heidt, ducking the steaming white avalanche, then recoiling in horror as he saw it flow over the edge of the table into the basket. Soon the basket was overflowing with cereal and there was a horrible stench of something burning, a futile thrashing inside. Stillness.

A swaying Bond, steadied by Goshen and Neon, pointed a finger at the basket. "Dump it out on the table."

Gasps flew throughout the *La Guerre* Room as the basket was turned over and the cooked cereal-saturated body of Locksley, the dwarf, fell onto the baize with a spongy thump, the puckered baked apple of a face in the horrifying attitude of death.

And with the dwarf and the cascading Cream of Wheat was something else—dozens of sodden aces of spades. Israel Bond spread them out and issued a clarion cry:

"Yo declaro coup de cheato; ergo, yo conquero banco!"

"Cheat! Cheat! Cheat!" The shouts barraged Heinz Sem-Heidt's ears. "Coup de cheato!"

"Which means, Nazi, according to the rules of Scarne, the whole kit and caboodle is mine—quasars, colodnys, the five-pack of Muriel Cigars in your lapel pocket, plus any decent phone numbers in your little black book. You're out of business. I've just kicked your organization on its TUSH. Take 'em all, Monroe."

The blob began to weep as the CIA team fanned out and covered the seven other German directors. "She will kill me! If you don't protect me, she will kill me!"

Goshen ordered his men to clear the room. He gave it straight to the teary Sem-Heidt. "We'll give you the fullest protection, Nazi, if you spill the beans about TUSH's plot against the king and Judaism. Otherwise, you're free to walk out right now. 'Course, Auntie might——"

"Nein! Nein!" The piggish eyes rolled in anguish. "I hate her! I have always hated her! I only married her because of her superior family background. Ja, I talk."

"I'm going upstairs, Monroe," Bond said. "Neon, Jimbo, come with me."

In his absence the CIA team's Bell & Howell sound camera was grinding, recording for posterity fifty thousand feet of lachrymose confession. In a few hours excerpts of it would be spotlighting the newscasts of Cronkite, Huntley-Brinkley and Jennings and, via Telstar, the rest of humanity. And thanks to Seymour Feig, Bond's press agent buddy who had negotiated a fast deal, it might also end up as a one-hour spectacular sponsored by Xerox, "TUSH, The Heil-Heilabaloo World of Neo-Nazism," with possible narration by Peter Ustinov and Leslie Gore.

A helluva night's work. Goshen smiled. The cabal exposed, Sahd Sakistan secured for democracy, thanks again to the greatest espionage weapon of all time, Israel Bond.

His joy was not shared by the dark, cruelly handsome "weapon" on the roof nor by 113 and James Brown, who watched the baleful yellow eyes glaring back as the helicopter climbed over the wall. Auntie Sem-Heidt and Dr. Ernst Holzknicht had escaped.

26. The Tale Of The Little Princess

When the eye-opening call came from M., Bond was on the moon-bathed dune with Sarah Lawrence of Arabia, his head in her golden lap, his mouth open to receive the Joyvah jells and Philly Greenwald Concord grapes dropping from her fingers. Their second physical fusion had been matchless ecstasy-squared, though she had again refused to lower her veil. "Not until our wedding night, dearest. And I hope you will be pleased to learn that I have memorized all of Hillel's commentaries, the writings of Peretz, Sholom Aleichem and the Singers, and six of Alan King's best routines. I shall soon be well acquainted with the rich diversity of Jewishness."

The beeper in the parked MBG sounded a Mem alarm and the voice of his Number One in Jerusalem unfolded the shocking contents of a cardiogram—a telegram that comes from the heart—sent to her c/o the Ministry of Defense.

Dear M., my beloved enemy; soon to be, I pray, my devoted friend:

I wish to surrender myself to you personally and confess all my sins. It is all too clear that God is on your side, M. How else to explain the crushing of our TUSH by the heaven-strengthened hand of Israel Bond? I suppose I should have remained at Shiv's to take my medicine, but Dr. Holzknicht, who witnessed my husband's debacle at the *la guerre* table via closed-circuit television, convinced me to flee with him. Since then we have parted company. I am hiding out in the Cissbah in Sahd Sakistan. Where Ernst has gone I truthfully cannot say, but I know he is planning an even ghastlier operation against the fine Jewish people, 'Operation End-All,' details of which I will be happy to furnish you as proof of my sincere contrition.

We are two old women, M., who should be playing mah-jongg together and fondling fat cherubic grandchildren instead of locking wigs in mortal combat. Let us forget the unpleasantness of the past and unite in genuine sorority. Enclosed is a map showing a suggested rendezvous point three nights hence. Please bring only one other person with you, as I shall be accompanied by my last servant, a harmless Monagro.

Hoping you'll find it in your heart to come and accept my apologies for any inconveniences I may have caused you and your People of the Book, I remain,

Gerda Sem-Heidt

* * * *

When Bond arrived at the airport, Op Chief Beame, his face mirroring his distrust, was wheeling the smiling M. down the special ramp built by the El Al technicians. There's something messianic in those warm eyes, Bond noted, and it's driven away her common sense.

He could hold it in no longer. "M., it's a trap!"

"Damn right," Beame said, chewing on his White Owl. "I've begged her, Oy Oy Seven, but she won't listen."

M. patted their heads with her careworn hands. "Mine dear boys, always worrying about a mother. It does my heart good to see your filial agony. It's what I live for. No, *boychiklach*, I must go to this fallen wretch and redeem her. And from a security standpoint, which I'm sure you think I have overlooked in my zeal, it behooves us to familiarize ourselves with any new Holzknichtian deviltry before he has an opportunity to execute it. If it is a trap, we must take that chance. You will accompany me, Oy Oy Seven. Whatever happens, you must swear not to interfere."

He did, the vibrations from his cracking knuckles splintering the crystal of his Kissling.

Bond polished off three cartons of Raleighs during the ride to the Cissbah, placing coupon after coupon in M's hands. He could see her sweet, serene face in the mirror, an unspoken prayer on the lips. The sun was sinking and from the minaret came the final call of the muezzin: "Hey, you—yes, *you,* you snotty young Allah-Is-Dead crowd over there—move aside and make room for pray-ers, make room for pray-ers!"

Number 10 on the Street of the Jaundiced Jackals was a one-story warehouse-type edifice with YUSEF LATEEF'S SCHOOL OF MODERN FLUTE in faded letters on the door. He unlashed the wheelchair from the MBG's roof, placed M. on the seat and kicked the door open, wheeling her into blackness. Somehow he found a wall switch and flicked it, a single naked bulb casting a weak light in the empty, soundless room. On the floor he saw a large roach and he smoked it up in three mighty inhalations to allay his nervousness.

A door on the opposite side of the building creaked open and there was a squeak of wheels across the earthen floor. Now he could see two mad-dog yellow circles coming out of the blackness and a chalk-white face radiant with triumph, which told his palpitating heart that Auntie Sem-Heidt was in no penitent mood, a fear confirmed by the presence of the swarthy, grinning Monagro (a rare breed, indeed) with knives stuck into his thick leather belt.

"So, filthy Judischer mongrels; you have come."

There was distress in M.'s face. "Those are hardly the words of a woman seeking her way back to mankind, Gerda."

"Ha-ha! You doddering fool! Did you nourish the hope that I, Gerda Sem-Heidt, would grovel before Jews? Die, Mother Margolies, die!"

"M!" Bond heard his warning shout melt the fine-grained wax in his ears as he swung her wheelchair out of Auntie's line of fire, but he was a shade too slow. Auntie's right claw touched a button on the battery in her lap. Something streaked from the right armrest of her wheelchair, a steel projectile which nosed into M.'s right shoulder. Now a pain was searing his own right shoulder; he looked dumbly at the Monagro's knife, fell to his knees. He could see the roseate glow leaving M.'s face and hear the grinding of her false teeth. Hold! Hold! he pleaded with the Poli-Grip in her dentures. Hold and preserve her dignity in her last moments!

Auntie's claws smacked together in fierce joy. "Just the first round, my Chosen People. Chosen, yes, for death. Ha-ha!" She nudged the Monagro. "A droll joke, eh, Cagliostro? Chosen for death. Hee-hee!"

Gevaldt! thought Bond; Auntie's "hee-hee!" is even more bloodcurdling than her "ha-ha!"—not that there's much blood left in me to curdle. Up, up, he expostulated to his body, up! He braced himself against M.'s wheelchair and felt the knife fall out of his shoulder, a torrent of claret hot upon its hilt. He saw M. swallow hard and press her Korvette's gauzeroy handkerchief, the one he'd given her for her eighty-fourth birthday (alas, she looked years older now) against her spouting wound.

"Gerda, I should like your permission to tell you a few things that are in my heart." M.'s request was almost inaudible.

"Ha ha! Behold the things in *my* heart instead! Behold!" The claws tore away the housedress. Bond squeezed his eyes tight. I'm craven, craven, he told himself, but I can't stand to see it again. He could not see (a fitting penalty for his cowardice) that M. did not flinch at the mechanical wonder on Auntie's body.

"It is a fine heart," M. said. "I know it must give you a great deal of pleasure, Gerda. Now, may I tell you of the things in mine?"

"Talk, creator of vile, reeking chicken soup. It will amuse me to hear the blatting of a trapped Jew. Do not think for a moment that I shall soften my heart—" she sniggered at her inside joke—"as Pharaoh finally did for Moses." Auntie turned to the Monagro. "I can see you are impatient, my pet. Hold off yet a moment before I bestow upon you the pleasure of cutting the great Oy Oy Seven's throat."

"Thank you, Gerda. I should like to give you the synopsis of a Shirley Temple movie I had the pleasure of watching."

M. started in a shaky fashion, painting a word picture of a dear curlyhead of a moppet in a frilly frock and blue hair ribbon whose Mums had passed away, her adoring, dashing Daddy, a soldier of Good Queen Victoria, and the love they held for one another. M.'s voice seemed to regain its resonance as she described long walks through the drowsy green beauty of an English summer day, the father's eyes softening with tenderness at the sight of his "little princess" gamboling across the meadow, picking a nosegay here, petting a fluffy rabbit there, skipping across the flat stones of a clear, burbling stream. Bond, his eyes still fastened, could see it all . . . the glances of affection between father and moppet, the thistles rustling in a gentle breeze.

Then M.'s voice drooped. The trumpets of war had sounded to shatter the idyllic life. Daddy was called to fight with his regiment in a strange, hostile land. With no kith or kin, he was forced to leave his golden-tressed angel in the care of a boarding school headmistress who assured him the child would find it warm and friendly.

Long, lonely days for a shy little girl, unable to fit in with the haughty daughters of noblemen, lightened infrequently by letters from Daddy, which she would read a thousand times to her lone friend at the school, Singh Dennis-Singh, the Hindu who served as the butler and polo coach. Then the dark day when the telegram arrived: "Your father, Sergeant Major K., of the Fifth Scottish Black Watch Grenadiers, has been taken prisoner by the cruel mountain tribes and is presumed to have been tortured to death."

"Stop! Stop! You filthy Jewish bitch!" The iron voice cut in like the Monagro's knife.

Bond, not knowing why M. had chosen this soulful narrative, awaited the worst, but suddenly he heard the Monagro's voice, heavy with emotion, intrude: "Let her continue, Gerda. Please let her continue."

M., pale and uncertain, her hand still pressed against the wound, went on.

Realizing the child was penniless, the headmistress forced her to vacate her cheerful room and take up residence in the garret, where she shared a closet with a dozen noisy shrews. "You will work in the scullery, *little princess*," the headmistress decreed, and so the golden girl toiled over pots and pans twenty hours a day, her little hands turning scabrous. In restive dreams she would see Daddy smiling. "The bloody beggars have been a bit hard on me, little princess. I've got only an eye and a leg left, but, never fear, I'll get home someday." He would, too, he would, she told Dennis-Singh who had climbed up with her gruel, "and it'll be like it was before, you'll see."

Bond heard the Monagro's deep, convulsive sobs and, without looking, knew the man's face was covered by his hands. "Goodbye, Gerda. I'm going to see a priest." The Monagro's feet pounded on the earthen floor and he heard the door slam.

"Come back, you half-breed cretin!" It was the iron voice. "I warned you, you Judischer scum! Now——"

A second rocket was ejected from the wheelchair and Bond winced, expecting to hear M.'s death wail, but he heard its harmless thud into the wall and her strangely composed voice resume the tale.

On a depressing night when the golden girl lay tossing with fever, the sad-eyed Hindu at her bedside, the headmistress threatening a caning for feigning illness, there came a knock on the garret door.

"Yes, yes, yes?" The voice of Auntie Sem-Heidt, wheezing and breathy, iron no more.

"Through that garret door," said M., her own voice quivering, "came an eye and a leg wrapped in the scarlet coat of a Grena——"

"Daddy! Daddy! Daddy! It's her Daddy. . . . Oh, oh, oh!" It was Auntie, screeching and sobbing. "Daddy! Daddy! Da——"

A protracted hiss, the pungent smell of something burning, a ghastly strangling cough——

He could bear his self-imposed blindness no longer. His eyes went first to M., a regretful smile on her dry lips, then to the sprawled-out scarecrow across the room. A greenish, rigid tongue had forced the blue-vein lips apart; though the yellow eyes were open, they saw not. He shuddered at the Dali-esque nightmare of the squidlike thing, its molten tentacles slowly spreading from its white-hot center.

Auntie Sem-Heidt was dead. Her heart had melted.

27. Ain't That A Kick In The Glass!

"Damn it," Bond fumed. "These long tapering fingers have time and time again kept the world safe for democracy. Now they can't even push a rose into the slit of a lapel."

"First of all, Mr. Nervous *Chulairyeh*," laughed Neon Zion, "it goes in by the stem, not the blossom. Secondly, you're *tzittering* like a child; let me do it."

Israel Bond *was* nervous. He was in the Empire State Building suite of Muhammud Ali-Shurmahn, Sahd Sakistan's ambassador to the U.S., and this sunny day in June was his wedding day. Minutes ago he had been on the 86th floor's open-air terrace to witness the splendiferous coronation of Baldroi LeFagel, who months back had insisted Bond share his memorable day by marrying Sarah Lawrence of Arabia immediately afterward. Hell, Bond mused, this thing is hairier than that windup with Auntie in the warehouse.

Op Chief Beame's Aleph-Priority response to his frantic beeper had saved M. and himself. He'd rushed them to the Jewish court physician, Dr. Chayim Khayam, who'd administered plasma, Mother's Activated Old World Germicidal P'chah and four vital Excedrins. Sarah paid daily visits to the recuperating pair with armloads of Uneeda Biscuits and read verse to them from Bond's favorite, "Best of Hallmark." M., curt at first, had finally fallen under Sarah's spell. "You're a good *shikseh;* if you'll convert I'll come to the wedding." The veiled beauty kissed the fragile hand. "Smashing! M., old girl! I shall, indeed. Since I last saw Mr. Bond, I have memorized *Jews, God and History,* the songs of Shoshana Damari and Theodore Bikel, the speeches of—"

"Cool it, baby. M. says you're in."

With the joint news release by the Tall Texan and Ambassador Callowfellow that America was going to host the coronation of its native son turned king, the country had gone gaga. LeFagel Bagels, shaped like a crown, began popping up in every Jewish-owned establishment (they'd all been rebuilt by the Tall Texan's crash program, Operation Help-A-Hebe). Imperial Margarine had donated the royal crown (beating a disgruntled soda company to the punch) for the fete. A particularly clever tobacco firm inserted a full-page ad in *The New York Times:* "Roi-Tan Loves You, King Baldroi, 'Cause You're the Roi and You're Tan." LeFagel's "We Should Think About Spoons" vaulted to No. 1 on the best-seller list; he benefitted further from a commercial tie-in with 1847 Rogers Brothers Silver, which gave the book free with every 42-piece set of spoons. (People did not seem to want anything but spoons; it was considered passé to eat steak with a fork these spoon-fad days.)

LeFagel's party arrived to a tumultuous New York welcome; a lavender line was painted down Fifth Avenue by his adoring claque from the old "angry poet" days. He seemed distant in their presence, however; one spying his bulky Julius Boros plus-fours cried: "Sellout!"

There had been a final soul-searching dialogue with LeFagel an hour before the coronation.

"Sixty minutes from now, Oy Oy Seven, I shall be king, but I'd give it all up—power, fame, money—if you'd consent to go away with me. What say you, captor of my heart?"

Bond put his arm around the little king. "You've made tremendous strides, Baldroi. When first we met, you were a screaming faggot. Step by step I've seen a miracle unfolding. Now, I don't know too much about these things, but I'd guess you have roughly 7.9 percent homo left in you, a bit higher than the permissible 6 percent in most men, but certainly manageable with a little effort. Fight it hard all the way. Your people need a man at the helm. For their sake, think manly, talk manly, do manly things."

LeFagel left him with a grim smile and Neon rushed back to Bond ten minutes later with a bulletin: LeFagel had assaulted a shapely female researcher from *Sh-h-h* Magazine.

Good-o! Bond thought. My work is done. He's a *mensch!*

A richly humorous incident had stamped the Tall Texan's warm, human brand on the formalized proceedings. He and the king had posed for the TV cameras performing a hallowed Sakistani rite, the salting of each other's *shasheeshah* (tails of spring lambs ground up with Cheerios) as a sign of mutual respect between world titans. Bond had whispered something to the Tall Texan, who whispered back, "Right fine, son. I'll say it," then lifted the saltcellar and cracked up the crowd with a sly, "Come, your Majesty; let us *season* together." Bond had refused the Tall Texan's offer of a high-level speechwriter's job, but exacted a promise that the latter would give Monroe Goshen a salary hike far above the Administration's 3.3-percent guideline, which everybody was ignoring anyway.

Borne to the throne by two Kurds and two Wheys in a Norman Hekler-designed four-door sedan chair, LeFagel, dressed in blinding white Labrador snow-goose feathers and tennis sneakers, took the crown from Ben-Bella Barka's hands and, crying out three times "Y'llella abdabeel" (Sakistani for "I am crying out three times"), placed it on his head. He then left for dinner with the Tall Texan. "Put Mr. Bond's wedding on the bill, too, huh, Prez?" LeFagel had said. Now the hundreds of dignitaries and security people were gone; only a handful were left for the nuptials. M., knitting madly, put the finishing touches to Bond's wedding yarmulke. Milton and Rag and their wives sat next to her.

And alone in the back row was Liana, lovely and brave. She'd made a pretext of fixing his zipper to talk to him. "Iz, I know she's a lovely girl, but if it doesn't work out, I'll be waiting."

"How long? Don't make commitments of fidelity you can't keep, like last time," he said a little too harshly.

"Forever."

He seemed appeased. He stood at the mesh railing looking at the breathtaking panorama of the world's most exciting depressed area 1050 feet below, waiting for his bride.

Rabbi Howard Hinderstein, head of the somewhat liberally oriented congregation Temple B'nai Venuta, who had been recommended to M. by friends, was shamefully late, profusely apologetic. "Coronation traffic, you know, Mr. Bond." He waved in two workmen who wheeled the portable wedding canopy (*huppah*) onto the terrace. It was quite tall, about nine feet, and was constructed of aluminum and bedecked with thousands of posies. He had them position it at the spot where the red carpet abutted a wall. Then he put his finger to his lips and the small assemblage hushed.

Goshen, Neon, Op Chief Beame and James Brown, acting as ushers, helped the unsteady groom down the carpet as the accordion player squeezed out *Because of You,* halted it after a few bars, fooled around with *Because You're Mine,* stopped again, consulted a sheaf of music and then went into *Because,* the onlookers aah-ing with relief. "Turn around, Iz," said Goshen. "You've got company."

She came, Latakia's soft padded feet leaving four-inch indentations in the rug. From the first notes of her theme song he knew she had made an irreparable break with her past for his sake. The notes were the same, but now the tape rolled out a special new version by a cantor: *dai dai, bime, bime, bime, bime, dai dai. . . .*

From that moment on, his grey eyes hypnotized by her bottomless black pools peeping over the veil, he was in a dream, somehow managing to repeat woodenly what was asked of him by Rabbi Hinderstein. A voice in the dream said, "Ring? Mr. Bond? Ring! Ring! Ring!"

He heard himself say: "Somebody answer the phone." Goshen chuckled, took the nearly tenth-of-a-carat garnet ring from his pocket and placed it in Bond's feeble fingers.

"Now," said Rabbi Hinderstein, "the ceremonial breaking of the glass to remind us of the destruction of our temple in ancient times and the bitterness of life we must endure." Bond's eyes struggled to focus on the rabbi's hand as it placed the glass near his feet. "Break the glass, Mr. Bond," said the amused spiritual leader. Bond drove his Angora bedsock down hard and sent Goshen hopping off with a crushed big toe. "Again, Mr. Bond." Loathing himself for the simpering grin he knew marred his cruel, darkly handsome face, Bond stepped down again, missing by a wide margin.

"Iz, you dotty, frightened boy! I'm not going to be unlawfully yours a single moment more. This is a job for *Mrs.* Israel Bond." With a sparkling laugh Sarah Lawrence of Arabia Bond lifted her well-turned leg. "No! No!" It was the Rabbi, inexplicably enraged. Down came the foot and her soft-soled ballerina splintered it resoundingly. "There, that's done. Hold me, my lovely, lovely husband. Oh, I'm going to—"

She crumpled to the red carpet. Now the smog of fear was burned off his mind; he sprang to her side and cradled her head in his arms. The uncovered part of her face was blue.

"Dear, dear. The excitement, I suppose." It was Rabbi Hinderstein calming the shocked wedding guests. "See to her, dear people. I'll roll the *huppah* away to give the poor child some breathing room." He put his shoulders against a side and guided it toward the terrace's railing.

"Sarah, my love." His eyes hot and salty, Bond pulled away her veil to administer mouth-to-mouth resuscitation, then froze.

AIN'T THAT A KICK IN THE GLASS!

Sarah Lawrence of Arabia's upper lip was adorned with a thick, black, neatly trimmed military moustache. She mumbled in a dying voice, "Curse of all female cousins, twenty-fourth to forty-eighth, related to Lawrence by marriage . . . 'the Lawrence Lip' . . . imbalance of hormones . . . must shave daily . . . didn't want you know 'till married . . . so sleepy . . . so. . . ."

The smell from the shards of glass! Yes, *gorgogga,* the pancreatic juice of the *varapapa* frog of the Honduran swamps; no deadlier venom had ever existed.

She was gone. He knew who was responsible.

"Holzknicht, you —— kraut fiend!"

From the *huppah,* which had suddenly acquired a seat that held Rabbi Hinderstein, came a flash, and hot metal creased his scalp. "Die, Bond! This is Nazi Germany's revenge!"

"Iz!" Goshen yelled at the top of his lungs. "Take my gun. *You* finish the sadistic bastard." As Goshen slung the snub-nosed Tiniff .44 across the floor to the flattened-out Israeli, Dr. Ernst Holzknicht, who had so brilliantly played his part, cut the CIA op chief down with three slugs.

Then from the top of the canopy emerged rotor blades, whirring, lifting it slowly. The traditional canopy of a Jewish marriage was a garlanded helicopter!

Throwing all caution aside, Bond made it to the rising chopper in six unbelievable leaps and squeezed the fingers of his left hand around the circular steel frame to which the three wheels were attached, shoved the gun into the pocket of his Sunkist orange tuxedo and grabbed another six inches of the bar with his right. Doktor Holzknicht, three feet above him, thrashed out with his Heidelberg bedsocks in an attempt to smash Bond's fingers, scoring a glancing hit on the right hand, but he was forced to pay attention to the controls, for now the chopper was high over the terrace, fighting for altitude against the pull of Bond's weight. The Israeli felt the wind, so deceptively gentle on the terrace, become a dangerous Hydra-headed force, buffeting him this way and that, and he squeezed harder. Up went the chopper—the 94th floor, the 99th; he looked down and saw death beckoning from the street some 1200 feet away. . . .

It was over the very tip of the Empire State Building's TV tower that the scientist exploded his next trick. He pushed a button that jettisoned the circular frame. Now Bond was falling from the underpinnings of the craft, Holzknicht soaring away with a savage laugh.

"Auf Wiedersehen, jüdischer dumbkof!"

Gottenu! Bond fell toward the tower, then with a divine inspiration, thrust the steel ring over the slender TV tower tip and came to a teeth-rattling stop.

Ringer!

He had made himself a living quoit.

ON THE SECRET SERVICE

The impact bent the tower, which began to rock sickeningly back and forth, but he held fast. Close your eyes, fool! Don't look down until you've regained your equilibrium or you'll surrender to a mad urge and let go. Think about something else. He thought about the terrible reception the area's millions of TV viewers were getting this very instant because of the swaying tower. Bet the Mets *really* look shaky now, his sardonic wit told him.

There was a clatter above—Holzknicht, stunned by Bond's coup, circled back for the kill. Bond released his right-hand grip on the steel ring to fish Goshen's gun from the tux. He bit a sensual lip as the chopper zeroed in. Why doesn't Herr Doktor open up with his machine gun? I'm defenseless against it. The pht-pht-pht of the blades gave him the grim answer. A last bit of Aryan sport. Holzknicht wanted to maneuver the craft in such a way that the blades would. . . .

Now! You'll have only one chance, buddy boy. Bond, his clothes flapping in the blade-made breeze, put a single shot into the copter. He hadn't aimed for Holzknicht; it was the machine he had to stop before it shredded him into Cohenfetti. Not a bad line, he smiled, considering where I am.

He heard the first sputter, then a violent choking sound, and knew he had hit the control box and severed vital wires.

The doctor was frantically climbing out of the chopper; smoke began to curl ominously. Then Holzknicht leaped onto the tower, but he failed to grab it solidly and began a long slide toward Bond. "Die with me, Jüde!" His feet came down ponderously on the hand in the ring and Bond screamed; his bloody squashed fingers released it. They were falling together.

Even as he fell, Holzknicht's hands moved to throttle Bond and the latter felt nails tearing at his neck, then slipping off as a crosscurrent swept the falling Nazi away from him.

The air rushed through Bond's nose and ears; he could hardly catch his breath. He fell headfirst past the 86th floor and heard M.'s heart-rending cry, down, down, past the 75th, where his face was spotted by a curvaceous brunette in a window, BLOCH & TACHLE, MARINE LAWYERS, whose eyes lit up in recognition. Yes, Hillary Katzenellenbogen, she of the unforgettable weekend at Brown's Hotel in the Catskills, the body beautiful who had won the "Miss Jerry Lewis' Favorite Resort" swimsuit title; be true to me, sweet Hillary; goodbye . . . past the 46th, KELSEY KOMPUTERS . . . hell, he owned a hundred shares of that! And it's going up, up . . . and *you're* going down, down, his wit needled him again; the 32nd . . . just a few more seconds, Oy Oy Seven, and that lithe, muscular body you prize so will be a stinking mess of smashed atoms on the 34th Street sidewalk . . . the 25th . . . at least the f——ing kraut goes with me; I hope you're watching him blubbering as he falls, Sarah, my darling; the 19th . . . hey, TANTAMOUNT PICTURES is holding a screening of *The Dead Lay Wounded on the Road to Smolensk;* not bad; I saw it at the Cannes Film Festival . . . the leading lady was better in my bed than she was in the leading man's . . . Sonia, I'll miss you . . . the 12th, 9th, 5th, it's coming, Oy Oy Seven, the cement that'll disintegrate you into . . . 3, 2, 1 . . . pain, pain, pain. Israel Bond crashed into something huge and black and his fall to glory was over.

Epilogue

Trivia Festival Week, that annual excursion into the nostalgia of yester-year, was in full swing. At the Hotel Statler the Orphan Annie Fan Club crowded into a suite to sing:

> *"Who's that sloppy little mess?*
> *"Who wears that same ol' goddam dress?*
> *"Who can it be?*
> *"It's Little Orphan Annie!"*

The oldest member, a Miss Hecate Sensenbaugh of Omaha, was given the coveted privilege of barking "Arf! Sez Sandy" at the appropriate moment in the song, not so much in deference to her golden years as for the fact that she possessed a pair of lidless, lashless, pupil-less eyes. The new Lincoln Center for the Performing Seals housed a tremendous Trivia contest attended by 12,000 Triviaddicts, the very best of all an Elmo (Mr. Total Recall) Trickypepper of Shortweight, Oklahoma, who remembered that it was Tastee-Yeast who sponsored Jack Dempsey's *My Battle With Life*. At the Americana the Tisch clan hosted the Bobby Benson bunch; the Donald Meek fans, every bit as fastidious as their hero, ate watercress sandwiches on paper plates and tittered at each other at the Warwick; the Johnson Family and Amos N' Andy Fan Clubs, gathered at Marsal's at the Brevoort, made two historic decisions: (1) to merge; (2) to accept Negro members.
tittered at each other at the Warwick; the Johnson Family* and Amos Fan Club outdoor conclave on 34th Street. The president, made up and costumed to emulate the rugged film star, took off his pith helmet and led the members in the somber recital of the immortal old line: "It

---

* Not the stars of the Kenny Solms—Gail Parent "Great Society" LP, but a "radio family," all played by one very clever impressionist. If you recall his name, you rank up there with Elmo Trickypepper—S.W.

wasn't the airplanes that got him; oh, no. 'Twas Beauty who killed the Beast." They whispered "Amen" and boarded the bus in silence.

So it was that a few minutes later the sorrowing M. led Latakia and the other crushed, tearful wedding guests out of a side entrance, not knowing that Oy Oy Seven had landed upon the fifty-ton Andy Warhol-designed, foam-rubber replica of King Kong, who himself had taken the terrifying plunge off the world's tallest structure in the 1933 film classic.

Israel Bond, waist-deep in rubber and matted fur, was bloody and battered—understandably—but very much alive. There was no elation in his heart, for he had seen the warped genius who had taken his own true love's life bounce off the simian's skull into the back of a beer truck making its way toward—God only knew. His lips twisted into a moue of irony as the grey eyes saw the brand name on the beer truck— Lowenbrau. And they say *we're* clannish, he thought bitterly.

There'll be a day of judgment, mein lieber Doktor Ernst Holzknicht. We'll cross trails again.* Maybe on an Alpine mountaintop, on a burning desert, in some impenetrable rain forest (to be truthful, I hope it isn't a rain forest. My rain-forest attire is the least stylish part of my whole wardrobe), on a frozen tundra or across a crowded room. And once I have found you, I'll never let you go.

* In the last Israel Bond thriller, *You Should Only Live and Not Die— Altogether,* from the Papermate Pen of Sol Weinstein, a wonderful person altogether.